Aware
of the
Wolf

Dedication

David:
Aunt Margaret, Uncle Louie, and P.D.

Charlie:
Mary and Mason

ISBN 978-0-9728461-7-2

Printed in the U.S.A.

First Printing, March 2007

Aware of the Wolf
Table of Contents

Name Pronunciation Guide

In adventure books like Knightscares, some names will be familiar to you. Some will not. To help you pronounce the tough ones, here's a handy guide to the unusual names found in this book.

Erzua
Er - zoo - uh

Ithasuma
Ith - uh - sue - mah

Jasiah
Jay - sigh - uh

Moogla
Moo - glah

Necrowhal
Neck - row - wall

Octoclops
Ock - toe - clops

Octolith
Ock - toe - lith

Visit www.knightscares.com to hear the names pronounced on your computer by the authors.

Neverthaw

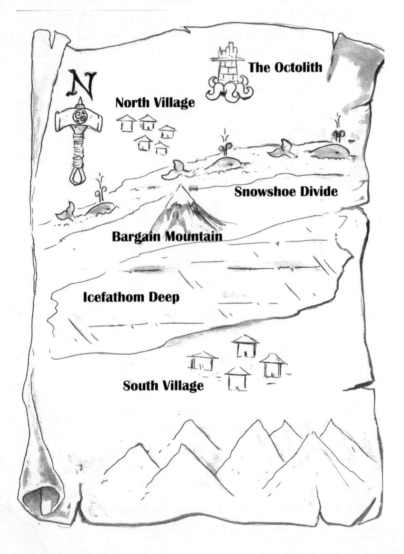

Knightscares #8:
Aware of the Wolf

David Anthony
and
Charles David

Winter Games

1

With a yelp, I dove headfirst into a snow bank just before the Winter Orb struck. Howling, icy wind shrieked over my back, but the Orb didn't touch me.

Skree-ee-ee!

To my left, Levi wasn't so lucky.

Thwalmp!

Levi did his best to catch the Orb, but it broke through his cupped hands and smacked him full in the gut. He toppled into the snow like a chopped tree, turning blue. The Orb bounced at his feet and went still.

"Out!" shouted the rule judge from the edge of the playing field. "Noah's throw."

I grimaced and stood up. I was Noah, and it was my turn to throw the Orb.

"Good luck," Levi gasped before freezing completely.

The Winter Orb was a blue and white swirled ball about

the size of a cantaloupe. It had caused some trouble down south recently, but here we used it to play a game. Those it struck were covered in a thin sheet of ice. They stayed that way until the end of the match.

I grunted at Levi and retrieved the Orb. My friend would be fine, but it would take a miracle for me to win. I had no business being one of the last two kids playing.

Across the field hunched Bart, the biggest, fastest, strongest boy in Neverthaw. He was also the meanest, and looked more like a bear standing on its hind legs than a ten-year-old boy.

As for me, I was the second-biggest kid in Neverthaw's South Village, but I wasn't very tall. My family used words like *solid* and *big-boned* to describe me. I just hoped my height would catch up with my weight soon.

My hair was shoulder-length, blond, and always in my face. Boys from Neverthaw were forbidden to grow it longer or to tie it back. Long hair was a symbol of adulthood, so everyone grew it as long as possible without breaking the rules.

I guess that made me an average kid, except for my size. But being solid and chubby had advantages. I could out-wrestle most other kids, and I could almost carry my father's magic hammer, Stormfall.

"You gonna throw or what?" Bart barked from across the icy field. Not only did he look like a bear, he snarled like one.

Instead of answering, I reared back and threw the Orb.

Skree-ee-ee!

My aim seemed good, and I had hopes that the throw would connect. The Orb flew fast. It flew straight. It flew right into the ground.

"Har, har!" Bart brayed, holding his ground while the Orb dribbled to a stop near his snowshoe-sized boots. "Nice throw, Naomi."

Hearing that, I groaned. Naomi was my sister, my *kid* sister. Bart had suggested that I threw like a little girl.

"Oh, go cut your hair!" Naomi shouted from the crowd of spectators standing around the field. The phrase was a serious insult to anyone from Neverthaw.

"Har, har!" Bart chortled again, never taking his beady eyes off me. "She shoulda played, not you." A murmur of chuckles swept through the crowd.

Thanks, Naomi, I growled silently, shooting her a chilly stare. She never knew when to keep her mouth shut. Now the crowd expected Bart to wallop me.

I feinted right and then sprinted left, hoping to confuse Bart. A cluster of frozen players huddled a short way off. They would make a good barricade if I could reach them in time.

Bart didn't seem to be in a hurry. He casually bent and scooped the Orb up with a big paw.

My boots crunched as I plodded across the snow. My breath puffed out in chalky clouds.

11

Just make it, I begged myself. *Survive for one more round. Don't let Bart humiliate you.*

When Bart cocked his arm, I jumped for all I was worth. Then he grunted and the Winter Orb was on its way.

2

My feet left the ground. I was flying. My arms stretched, willing me forward. I streaked like a spear toward the group of frozen players.

Big-boned me—a spear!

Skree-ee-ee!

The Winter Orb hurtled my way. Flying snow and sleet churned in its wake.

Come on, Noah, you can—! But I never finished the thought.

Blamphff!

It was another bull's eye for Bart. Numbing cold exploded in my right side as the Orb struck my ribs.

Teeth chattering, I groaned through blue lips and tumbled off course. Then I crashed heavily to the ground in a shower of snow.

The bigger they are, the harder they fall, I reminded

myself. The saying went double for me.

"Har, har!" Bart gloated. "I win again. I always win. Too bad, *Naomi*."

I wanted to stick my tongue out at him, but the Orb had frozen me stiff. All I could do was stare face first into the snow and think about how I'd lost—*again*.

Vwarrr-oooohnnn!

A horn trumpeted then, signaling the end of the game. The rule judge declared Bart the winner, and the crowd cheered loudly.

Because of his skill, Bart was always the favorite. It seemed that most people wanted to root for a winner no matter who it was. They certainly weren't cheering for Bart's bear-like manners or personality.

Naomi didn't cheer. She was as loyal to me as a hungry puppy looking for dinner. Sometimes that and her big mouth got her into trouble.

"Shouldn't you be hibernating?" she accused Bart. Then to the rule judge, "Judge? Judge! Since when are mangy bears allowed to play?"

For once Bart didn't laugh. He roared at me. "You're gonna get it, Noah!"

Correction: Sometimes Naomi's big mouth got *me* into trouble.

Water trickled into my eye, and I struggled to move. Now that the game had ended, the Orb's ice was thawing. I wiggled my toes, flexed my calves, and then pushed myself to my knees.

Naomi was immediately at my side. She was shorter and a lot thinner than I was, but you could tell we were related. She wore her hair in twin braids on the sides of her head like pigtails.

"Hurry, Noah," she urged. "Bart is up to something."

As I struggled to stand, I spotted Bart and his gang packing armloads of snowballs. None of his friends were as big as he was, but they made up for that with bad attitudes. They glared and grinned threateningly from across the field.

Naomi and I didn't wait or wonder. Their snowballs were meant for us. We started to creep through the crowd, but a strong hand gripped my shoulder and turned me around.

"You made your father and me proud," my mother said. The strong hand belonged to her. She was a tall woman with eyes like frozen tears.

Next to her, my father still looked like a giant. He was as muscular as I was chubby. Talk about big-boned!

"Soon you will be strong enough for Stormfall," he told me, patting the massive battle hammer he wore on his hip. The hammer was a family treasure passed from father to son. I couldn't wear it without dragging it through the snow.

"Bart won, Father," I protested.

My mother snorted. "No one in Bartholomew's clan can

count more than the fingers on one hand. His exact age is impossible to know."

She meant that Bart was probably older than the other players and I. That would give him a huge advantage. Why his parents would lie about his age, I couldn't imagine. Winning wasn't *that* important.

Right then, it didn't matter much. Bart and his friends were still packing their icy arsenal. And from the look of it, they were almost done.

"We have to go," I said rapidly, and Naomi nodded. "We'll see you at home."

Before our parents could respond, we dashed into the crowd. Bart and his crew followed immediately. The chase was on!

Bully Rush

3

Naomi sprinted lightly over the snow, leading the way. Her twin braids flapped behind her like pennons tied to a knight's lance.

I slogged behind, puffing hard after ten steps. I'd already had a tiring day, and I had just been frozen by the Orb. Plus, my body wasn't exactly built for running.

Behind us, Bart and his thugs hooted, giving chase. A few of their snowballs splattered in the distance. *Splart! Splert! Splet!* But we were too far ahead to hit … yet.

"You girls can't run forever!" Bart snarled, closer than I expected.

Naomi shouted back at him over her shoulder without slowing. "Stick your head in the snow!" Then she grabbed my elbow and turned sharply down a narrow trail to our left.

I almost planted my feet like a stubborn mule and refused

to budge. Naomi was crazy! The trail she had chosen was dangerous. It ran steeply downhill and into a dead end. A *deadly* dead end.

At the bottom of the hill lurked a foreboding woods. It bristled in a secluded valley surrounded by sheer icy walls on three sides. The only way out was the way in, so we would be trapped down there.

Worse, the woods was full of needlespine pines, a dangerous type of tree that grew in Neverthaw. I would rather face Bart and a hundred frozen snowballs than go near just one needlespine pine. Hugging a porcupine was safer!

"What's wrong with you?" I demanded of Naomi. "The needlespines will turn us into pincushions!"

My sister huffed in annoyance. "And Bart's snowballs will turn us into pancakes. What's your point, Noah?"

I sighed and dropped the subject. Bart would clobber us for sure, but maybe the needlespine pines would leave us alone. It wasn't likely, but there was a chance.

We staggered downhill through knee-deep snow. The trail was marked by the prints of animals, but no other people had come this way in a while. No one else was foolish enough to disturb the needlespine pines.

"Har, har!" Bart gloated, gaining on us. He knew we were in trouble and headed for more. "It's us or the pines, girls. What's it gonna be?"

Spluck! Splurk! More snowballs spattered the ground behind us, also gaining.

This time Naomi didn't respond to Bart's teasing. We had reached the bottom of the hill, and the icy woods silenced us. We stared at it, barely breathing.

The needlespine pines were as beautiful as they were dangerous. They were shaped like pine trees, but looked as if they had been made from blown glass. Their slender limbs reminded me of a skeleton's arms. When light touched them, they blazed with color.

When anything else touched them, they turned deadly.

Right then, the woods shone a disturbing blood-red hue. The sun was setting, and its fading light seemed to bathe the trees in fire. That couldn't be a good sign.

"*N*-now what?" I whispered, breaking our silence.

Naomi shrugged and tugged hard on a braid. Her grey eyes narrowed as she peered at the trees.

"We go in the woods, I guess," she answered at last. "I didn't think Bart would follow us this far. Not down here."

Her words angered me. "You should have thought about what could happen," I reprimanded her. "Now we have to go into the woods. We don't have a choice."

This time I grabbed her elbow and dragged her after me. She had led us to the woods hoping Bart wouldn't follow. But he had, and there was nowhere left to run.

We had to enter the needlespine pines.

Beeline For Needlespine

4

I kept Naomi close as we ducked into the woods. We didn't dare bump or brush even the smallest branch. The trees would fill us full of needles if we did.

That was the danger of the needlespine pines. They could fire their icy needles like stinging bees. They were also smarter than regular trees, and fiercely guarded their territory. If we touched one, all of them would attack.

For now the woods stood silent. We barely breathed as we took big, exaggerated strides. We high-stepped through the snow like marching soldiers. Walking that way made me feel silly, but I preferred living silly to dying seriously.

"Stop!" Naomi hissed suddenly, and I froze at the urgency in her voice.

"There." She pointed straight down at my feet.

In the snow where I had been about to step was a massive paw print. It belonged to a wolf but was twice as big as normal. A trail of similar tracks led farther into the trees.

"What kind of wolf makes prints that big?" I asked, almost groaning. *And why do things have to keep getting worse?*

Naomi shivered against me. *"Th*-that kind," she gasped in a strangled voice.

This time she didn't point at what she saw. She was too afraid. Not even the Winter Orb could have frozen her more. She stared unblinking into the eyes of the biggest wolf I'd ever seen.

The animal crouched to our right, its shaggy belly hanging just above the snow. Thick white fur coated its body, but both of its ears were solid black. Its wide head stood as high as my chest.

"S-t-a-y," I whispered slowly, knowing the wolf wouldn't understand. At the same time, I stepped backward and tugged on Naomi's parka.

Everything I knew about wolves told me to be calm. Wolves rarely attacked people. They were supposed to be more afraid of us than we were of them.

But this wasn't an ordinary wolf, and I was plenty afraid. This wolf was as big as a pony. I doubted that a chubby boy and his pigtailed little sister would scare it away.

The wolf watched us intently with yellow eyes. Slowly its powerful jaws opened, revealing sharp fangs.

"Come out, come out, wherever you are!"

Bart unknowingly both saved the day and made everything worse. Only he could do that at the same time.

When his gruff voice boomed behind us, the woods came instantly to life. A tinkling sound like ringing bells swept through the trees. Branches started to twitch and jerk. The trees were preparing to attack.

The noises got Naomi and me moving. We shared a quick glance then nodded at each other. We were going to have to take our chances with Bart and his friends. The pines were too dangerous now.

"Run!" I roared, giving up on stealth. Thanks to Bart, the trees knew we were here. There was no reason to waste time trying to be quiet now.

When I glanced up to start running, the wolf was gone. A fresh set of tracks streaked past us toward the edge of the woods.

At least something went right, I thought bitterly. Bart and the pines were enough. We didn't need a giant wolf after us, too.

"Move it!" Naomi bellowed, giving my shoulder a shove. "You make a nice target just standing there!"

Together we charged toward the trail, weaving through the trees. Branches and tree trunks quivered all around. The tinkling sound of stirring needlespines chimed louder, stinging our ears.

The needles were coming. We were going to be skewered like salmon swimming upstream.

Naomi sprinted in the lead again, and I chugged as close

behind as I could. Dark shapes darted through the trees, moving too rapidly to identify. Maybe the wolf hadn't given up after all.

Fffwitt! Thwing! Thwitt!

Then hundreds of icy needles were launched into the air. They hummed like mosquitoes and struck like sharpened splinters. Most bounced harmlessly off our thick clothing. Some found soft spots on our hands and cheeks.

"Cover—*ow!*—your eyes!" Naomi cried, whipping up the hood of her parka.

But I barely heard her. I was too busy feeling sorry for myself. Running long distances usually did that to me.

When will I be strong enough to carry Father's hammer? One swing of Stormfall would flatten these trees. I was tired of being overweight and under-muscled.

Ar-arr! Arrrr-roooo!

A blood-curdling howl interrupted my thoughts. It came from overhead, from somewhere in the trees. But how was that possible in this woods? Nothing I knew of could climb a needlespine pine.

Hardly thinking, I snatched Naomi's hood and dragged us to the ground. As we tumbled into the snow, I caught a glimpse of huge black wings dropping on us from above.

Arrrr-roooo!

The howl of a wolf pierced the night again, and the icy needles continued to fly. Then darkness fell over us, and I saw and heard nothing more.

Cloaked In Darkness

5

"Don't move," a rough voice growled in the darkness. "Don't even breathe."

I obediently held my breath, debating what to do next. Struggling would cause more needlespine pines to attack. Doing nothing could be even more dangerous. I didn't know anything about the person who had captured us.

And what makes you think it's a person? I asked myself doubtfully. From South to North Village, Neverthaw was home to many strange creatures. Most of them were definitely *not* people.

Time passed but I couldn't say how much. It felt like hours. It could have been minutes. Even Naomi kept quiet, and that was a surprise. She could be counted on to talk in her sleep.

When cold air washed over my face, I blinked my eyes open. The clear starry night sky spread out overhead. I was lying on my back in the snow.

"Who are you?" Naomi demanded in a harsh whisper. She was sitting on her knees, jabbing a mitten at someone I couldn't see.

I rolled onto my elbows and knees as quietly as I could. Needlespine pines still surrounded us. One startling sound could set them off again.

A dark figure wrapped in an even darker cloak squatted nearby. A hood was pulled over its head, hiding its face. Gloves covered its hands.

It's not too scary, I tried to convince myself. *At least it doesn't have two heads.* But I still didn't know what was under the cloak.

"I am not an enemy," the cloaked stranger said slowly. Its voice still had that rough edge, as if the speaker had a very sore throat.

I scooted closer to Naomi and put myself between her and the stranger.

"If that's true, then why is your face hidden?" I challenged.

"Yeah!" Naomi agreed, shouldering her way past me. "Show yourself. Who are you?"

The stranger exhaled loudly, and I thought I spotted sharp teeth inside the hood. Seeing them made we wish for my father's hammer more than ever. No one would dare bother us if I carried it.

"You're just like everyone else," the stranger snarled.

"When I saw you being chased, I hoped you were different. But Two-Shadows was right. You're all the same."

The stranger waved a hand and started to turn away.

"Wait!" Naomi hissed so emphatically that a nearby pine twitched in warning. "We're different," she promised, somewhat quieter. "And we can help."

I blinked at that, and the stranger rounded on her faster than a startled cat.

"Who asked for help?" it asked.

"Are you crazy?" I gasped at the same time.

To my dismay, Naomi giggled. It was a sassy little-sister sort of giggle. The kind she used when she knew she was right.

"Crazy runs in the family." She winked at me. Then to the stranger she said, "You saved us for a reason. At first I thought it was to eat us up. But since you didn't do that, you must need our help."

I blinked again. Sometimes Naomi was smarter than I liked to admit.

The stranger sighed heavily. The sound reminded me of a dog's whine. Then its shoulders and head drooped, looking tired.

Why is it so sad? I wondered, squinting into the hood. *And what's it hiding?* But most importantly, *Had I really seen the glint of teeth?*

After a pause, the stranger's head came up and its shoulders squared.

"My name is Ian," it rasped. "And that's all I can remember about myself. I need your help to break my curse."

With gloved hands, Ian slowly drew back his hood, and I
cried out in alarm at what I saw. The stranger had the hairy
grey and black face of a wolf!

6

This time I couldn't help making noise. I was too shocked to keep quiet. I was terrified.

"*Y*-you're a *werewolf*!" I cried.

The words were an accusation, not a statement. They told Ian that I didn't trust him. No way, no how. They told him to go away.

People didn't help werewolves. They ran away from them.

"Stay back," I warned, pulling Naomi closer to me. "We aren't afraid—"

Fffwitt! Thwing! Thwitt!

The needlespines attacked again, awakened by my outburst. Needles hissed through the air in an icy torrent.

I barely had time to throw up my arms before Ian was on top of us again. The black wings flashed again. So did his teeth. Then his cloak swept over us, and we were swallowed in darkness.

The three of us tumbled to the ground like circus clowns.
Ian fell on me. I fell on Naomi. My oversized body
mashed her into the snow.

"Get off me, oaf!" she snarled at me.

"Get off me, werewolf!" I snarled at Ian.

What fools we were! I hoped Bart and his friends
weren't watching.

Ian leaped to his feet as soon as the pines quit firing. A dusting of snow clung to his fur, and he quickly drew up his hood. I'm not sure if he did it because he was cold.

"Try to be quiet when you leave," he growled, turning and starting to walk away. "I won't save you again."

Naomi called after him. "That's right. We'll save *you* next time."

I slugged her in the shoulder, but not nearly as hard as I wanted to. "Stop it. Hush! We're going home."

As usual, she ignored me.

"We owe you, Ian," she continued. "We'll help you break your curse."

That stopped the werewolf in his tracks. His shoulders slumped and he froze, but he didn't turn around.

"You don't know what that means," he sighed. "You wouldn't even know where to start."

A knowing smile crossed Naomi's face. It was a smile that I knew too well. She had a plan, and I wasn't going to like it. Worse, she wouldn't take *no* for an answer.

"Oh, no," I mumbled helplessly.

"Dare me," Naomi challenged Ian.

Arrrr-roooo!

Suddenly the werewolf spun and raced back through the trees on all fours. Before I could scream, he snatched Naomi and me by our collars and started to haul us out of the woods.

Ian was amazingly strong. He was shorter and thinner

than I was, but he didn't have trouble dragging me around using only one hand.

No wonder so many people disliked werewolves. They were impossibly strong and fast. It was easy to dislike something that made you feel weak.

Beyond the woods, Ian plunked us down on the trail. But he didn't give us time to catch our breath or ask questions.

"Dare you?" he growled, tossing back his hood and fixing his yellow-eyed stare on Naomi. "I'm cursed! I don't remember who am I, and I've been turned into a werewolf! Do you know what that means?"

Naomi shrugged and pointed a mitten in his face.

"You don't scare me," she said. "But I can scare you."

Ian blinked and my muscles tensed. What could she possibly say that would frighten a werewolf?

"We're going to Bargain Mountain to see Erzua," she declared. "She knows everything. If there's a way to break your curse, she'll know it."

Hearing that, I tipped over into the snow. Erzua was a dragon. If she didn't scare Ian, nothing would. Just her name made my blood run cold.

Two Down, Five Uphill

7

"Now we gotcha!"

Suddenly everything went cold, not just my blood. Far-away dragons weren't all we had to worry about. There was Bart, too, and he was close.

He and his shady friends slouched uphill, looking like trouble up to no good. Their meaty hands clutched snow-balls the size of the Winter Orb.

"Har, har!" Bart laughed . His friends agreed, snickering in safety behind him.

Unafraid, Naomi leaped into action. She slipped past me and pointed daringly at the bunch.

"You'd better get out of here!" she said threateningly. "We've got a werewolf on our side."

Bart almost fell over with laughter. "A werewolf? Har, har! All I see is Big Mouth and Big Bones."

That was enough. Calling me names was one thing. A

lot of people did it. But Naomi was my kid sister and off limits.

"Ian," I said, turning. "Show him. Show—"

The words died on my lips. There was no sign of Ian. The boy werewolf had disappeared without leaving a trace.

"Where'd he go?" I asked in dismay. Without Ian, we were back where we had started. Our choices were to get clobbered by Bart, hide in the woods, or—

Stand and fight.

The idea came to me unexpectedly, surprisingly. We could stand and fight. We didn't have to run, and we didn't have to hide.

Most of all, it meant we didn't have to lose.

Stand and fight.

Sure, we were outnumbered and we would take our lumps. But Bart would take his, too. Maybe he would take so many that he would learn to leave us alone.

"Aim for Bear-Breath!" I shouted to my sister. To my surprise, she was already digging in the snow with both hands.

"Way ahead of you, Noah!" she hooted. "Let's make that grizzly as white as a polar bear!"

Big mouth or not, I liked her thinking.

Bart didn't. He shambled backward and glanced anxiously at his friends. He hadn't expected us to make a stand.

Maybe he's going to run, I dared to hope. *Maybe no*

one's ever stood up to him before. Maybe I should have—

Whatever Bart was about to do, he didn't. One perfectly thrown snowball changed his mind. It sped straight from Naomi's mitten to his nose.

Spwurk!

Bart's hands flew to his face and his eyes widened in shock. They reminded me of double exclamations points at the end of a sentence. There were tears in his eyes but anger, too. A lot more anger than tears.

"Get them!" he bellowed from behind his hands. His voice was muffled but not his meaning or his rage. The fight was on.

Snowballs whizzed through the air. Five from uphill, two from down. Then they became impossible to count. Both sides attacked too furiously.

"Take this!" snarled Bart as he whipped a huge snowball straight at my head, still covering his nose with one hand. "And that!" his snickering friend added.

"Eat ice!" I roared back, throwing with two hands.

The stupidity of our comments only got worse. We should have left the insults to Naomi. She was the expert.

True to our plan, Naomi and I targeted only Bart. Not all of our throws hit their mark, but plenty of them did. They struck his legs, his head, and everywhere in between.

I think they drove him crazy, too. Well, crazier, that is.

"Charge!" he suddenly shrieked, dropping his ammunition and turning on his friends. One by one he started to push and shove them downhill.

"Charge!" he shrieked again.

His friends obeyed slowly. Most just stared, confused and unsure of what to do. A few well-placed kicks got them moving.

In the meantime, we kept throwing. Bart was red in the face and white everywhere else. What a sorry mess! Some black and blue was on its way, too, I'd bet.

"That'll teach you to pick on us!" Naomi taunted. "Five on two, and you still can't win!"

That did it. That comment changed everything. Bart locked eyes with Naomi and growled like a real grizzly.

"It's your turn, Mouth!" he snarled. Then he joined his friends and charged downhill.

Just like that, the snowball fight ended. Throwing snow from a distance wasn't enough for Bart anymore. He wanted to be close and in our faces. He wanted to swing his fists.

"The trees!" I cried, dropping a snowball. "Get back into the trees!"

For once Naomi didn't argue. She saw what was coming and couldn't deny it.

Bart was out for blood. It was time to run.

No Honor Among Thieves

8

Skoonch! Skoonch! Skoonch!

My boots crunched through the snow. My breath huffed
in ragged gasps. I was running for all I was worth.

"Not going … to make it," I panted, arms pumping. "*T-
too far.*"

That was the truth. The woods was still a dark blob
ahead. I could hit it with a rock or snowball, but I wouldn't
beat anyone there in a race.

"Hurry, Noah!" Naomi shouted over her shoulder.

She was halfway to the trees, sprinting effortlessly. Her
feet barely skimmed the snow. Her breath barely plumed in
the air.

Easy for you to say, I silently grumbled. *You aren't big-
boned.* Like always, my size was holding me back. Would
things ever change?

Bart heard Naomi and figured it was his turn to boss me

around. "Give up, Noah!" he bawled. "You're too slow!"

Hurry up. Give up. How about everyone just plain old "Shut up!" I wanted to yell.

Bart was closer than I'd hoped, and I could almost feel him reaching for my collar. My mouth opened to scream, but a surprising sight stole my breath.

A swarm of snarling shapes sprang from the dusky darkness like ghosts. Glimpses of fur, fangs, yellow eyes, and muscle swept past. Then I saw only white.

Ian? I thought dazedly, tripping and going down hard. Powder erupted around me, but I thought I spotted the werewolf boy in the confusion.

Arrrr-roooo!

His howl confirmed it. Ian had come to our rescue again, and this time he wasn't alone. He had brought friends.

Five new voices joined his. Five howling, snarling, barking voices. Without a doubt, they belonged to wolves.

"Get up, get up!" Naomi urged, tugging on my shoulder. Her rosy cheeks reminded me of strawberry eat-a-gones. "Quick! They're running!"

"Who? The wolves?" I sputtered, floundering in the snow. Right then I felt the way a turtle must when it's been rolled onto its back. It knows it'll figure things out eventually but never soon enough.

Naomi heaved one last time. "Stand!" she grunted, and up I came.

"Oh, relax," I snapped at her. "I'm not *that* big." I

started to brush myself off, but she forcibly turned me toward the hill.

I blinked at the unexpected sight. Then I laughed.

Bart and his gang were running uphill as if their lives depended on it. They pushed and shoved each other like scrawny goblins fighting over table scraps.

Seeing them that way reminded me of the old saying: *There is no honor among thieves.* I guess it went for bullies too. When it came down to it, they even bullied each other.

Two shaggy wolves chased the boys, nipping at their heels. To the wolves, it was a game, not a real hunt. They ran just fast enough to keep the bullies scrambling.

Ian crouched casually next to us, also watching the wolves. He had his hood thrown back and was smiling. His large teeth made an even larger impression on me.

"Sorry it took so long," he growled sincerely. "Two-Shadows and the others were chasing rabbits."

Naomi caught on quickly. "Two-Shadows is the wolf with the black ears, right?"

Ian nodded. "She watches out for me. Without her, I ..." He shrugged and glanced down at his feet.

An awkward but brief silence followed. Then Two-Shadows loped over as if she knew we had been talking about her. Her tongue lolled out of her mouth in a wolfish grin, same as Ian.

Right away, I understood why Ian valued her friendship. Two-Shadows looked after him as if he were her cub. She was always close and ready to protect him.

The strangest thing happened next. Ian and the wolf faced one another and started to yip and growl. They even barked a few times. I couldn't be sure, but it almost sounded as if they were arguing.

Finally Ian nodded at Two-Shadows, satisfied. The discussion was over, but I wasn't sure who had won, or what it had been about.

"Those bullies won't bother you again tonight," Ian said to us in his raspy voice. "They climbed trees and our packmates are guarding the way down."

Naomi and I laughed at that. What a nice way to put it. *Guarding the way down.* Bart and his gang were stuck like treed kittens until the wolves decided to let them go.

What went up, it seemed, didn't always come down. At least not right away.

"How long will your friends keep them up there?" Naomi giggled breathlessly.

Ian wiggled his bushy eyebrows. The gesture was the werewolf way of making a silly face.

"Until you get home tonight," he answered. "We have a big day ahead of us."

My laughter turned into a long, loud sigh. In the excitement of the snowball fight, I'd forgotten about Naomi's promise.

We still had to take Ian to Bargain Mountain to see the dragon.

Eye On the Moon

9

Morning was a long time in coming. For hours the full moon hung outside my window like an unblinking eyeball. It stared at me and inspired dark thoughts.

How perfect, I observed more than once. *A werewolf shows up on the night of a full moon.* The timing reminded me of something out of a cheap horror story.

Still, the moon and werewolf weren't what really kept me awake for most of the night. I knew the moon wasn't really an eye, and Ian seemed like a nice person. He might even be a nice friend.

No, it was the dragon that kept me up. It was Erzua. When morning came, we would set off for her lair. It might be the last place we ever went.

"You awake?" Naomi asked from my doorway. She spoke in the kind of voice that pretends to be quiet but always wakes the friend who's sleeping over.

"Yeah, I'm up," I said without turning. There was no reason to look at her. She would be staring at me with her hands on her hips. Sometimes she forgot which of us was the oldest.

To my surprise, she grunted. "*H*-help me with this thing," she huffed.

What's it now? I wondered, rolling over.

Halfway up, I froze. Naomi was trying to lift Stormfall, my father's war hammer.

"Be careful with that!" I snapped. I didn't want her touching it. Someday the hammer would be mine.

Someday when I'm big-muscled instead of -boned, I reminded myself. *If that day ever comes.*

"Be careful yourself," she shot back. "Dragon breath couldn't hurt this thing."

She was exaggerating, but not by much. Stormfall was very old and had seen many battles. Small chips and dents scarred its surface, but it still shone like a dragon's scales. It was as long as my leg and twice as thick.

"Let me get it," I said. She and I could argue all morning. We had done so over less important things. But Ian was probably waiting, and it was best to hurry.

We bundled up and crept outside as quietly as falling snow. Naomi wore a fur backpack over her shoulders. I dragged Stormfall alongside me.

I wore the hammer on my belt the way a knight wears a sword, but I didn't look or feel very heroic. Stormfall's weight forced me to lean like a team of sled dogs. My face was probably red.

"Ian is meeting us at the docks," Naomi whispered. No one in our village was awake but us, and she wanted to keep it that way.

I grunted softly, saying nothing. Talking and dragging the hammer down the street would take too much effort.

Our family's boat was docked on Icefathom Deep, a vast ocean that hadn't thawed in fifty years. Across the frozen sea was North Village and Bargain Mountain, home of the dragon Erzua.

Naomi was one of the best sailors in South Village, maybe in all of Neverthaw. If anyone could get us to Bargain Mountain, it was her.

How lucky, I chuckled humorlessly. I could think of a hundred places I'd rather go than to see a dragon. Like back to bed for starters!

Ian spoke before we spotted him. He slipped from behind our boat like a shadow that had sneaked away from its source.

"Morning," he growled, hood pulled tightly over his head.

"Good morning!" Naomi beamed at him. She was thrilled to be starting such a grand adventure with a werewolf.

I grunted again and heaved Stormfall into our boat. I was less than thrilled, but didn't say so. We had a job to do, and

complaining wouldn't change that.

Our boat was called an icerigger. Like all boats in Neverthaw, it was made to travel across ice. It had metal runners on its underside like a pair of ice skates and big sails to catch the wind.

As soon as Naomi climbed aboard, she got serious. And by serious, I mean bossy. She made it clear that she was both captain and crew. Ian and I were cargo along for the ride.

Which was fine with us. We crouched out of the way, our backs against the rail, and closed our eyes. Naomi did all the work.

I almost relaxed before the icerigger started to move. Then its sails snapped above me and Naomi shouted.

"Off we go!" Her smile was fierce as she stared into the wind.

I took a deep breath and tried to share her excitement.

Next stop: Bargain Mountain.

Icefathom Deep

10

Skrrrch!

Blades grinding, our boat sped across the Icefathom
Deep. South Village faded into the distance. Ahead, the
world yawned flat and empty all the way to the horizon.

We're so small, I found myself thinking. *Like insects
crawling across a windowpane.* It was a new concept for
me. I'd never felt small in my entire life.

Out on the ice, I started to understand just how big the
world really was. No matter where I looked, it seemed to
go on forever. The sight was dizzying.

Suddenly uneasy, I scrunched down in the boat and
pulled my hood low. I didn't like feeling this small any
more than feeling too big.

"Isn't this great?" Naomi hooted at me.

She didn't share my discomfort. Her mittened hands
clutched the wheel like a ship's captain during a storm.

Her round cheeks glowed rosily, and she had never looked more alive.

Ian shared her excitement. He hung his head over the rail and stared wide-eyed at what lay ahead. His tongue lolled out of his mouth like a panting dog's.

Seeing him that way, I couldn't believe that he was only part wolf. *Mostly* wolf seemed more accurate. If humans could become werewolves, could wolves become were*humans*? Ian made me wonder.

Skrrrch!

Naomi suddenly cut hard to starboard, and the boat veered sharply right. Everything else went left, including me. My big-boned self slid heavily into Ian and mashed him against the rail.

"Yip!" he barked.

"Sorry," I grunted between clenched teeth, feeling embarrassed. Then to my sister, I snarled, "What's the big idea?"

She covered one eye with a hand and squinted at me with the other. "Simmer down, land lubber," she drawled like a pirate. "Ye best hold tight 'til ye get yer sea legs. Arrgh!"

Ian snicker-growled in my ear, smiling wolfishly. Somehow his tongue never left its spot down by his furry chin.

I hope your faces freeze like that, I sneered silently. And it would serve them right. Naomi stuck squinting like a pirate and Ian forever licking his chops.

For the rest of the morning and into the afternoon, Naomi kept us sailing straight. The cloudy grey sky overhead never changed. Neither did the flat, frozen landscape.

Throughout, I almost wished something would come along to liven things up. Maybe a prowling polar bear or a row of penguins waddling on the march. Anything but more empty horizon.

I didn't realize that we were in danger, especially not from where it came. As we sailed along, I never imagined that we were being hunted from below.

"What's that dark spo—?" Ian started to ask, pointing a paw down at the ice.

A heavy thump beneath us cut him short.

Waulnk!

It caused the boat to rock, and the crisp crack of ice pierced our ears. Then the sound splintered quickly away in every direction.

"Hold tight!" Naomi cried, more alive than ever. "We've got company!"

She cranked the wheel to starboard again, and the icerigger groaned, turning and tilting. Its left blade actually came up off the ice for one breathless moment.

This time I didn't complain, because I saw it, too. The dark spot Ian had seen. It was streaking just below the ice. It was streaking right at us.

I recognized it right away. "Necrowhal!" I bellowed.

The shadow belonged to one of Neverthaw's deadliest creatures. We couldn't outrun it, and it could swallow us whole.

Anchor's Away

11

"Faster, Naomi!" I roared. "It's gaining on us!"

I was hunkered down on the deck of the icerigger, lying as low as my big bones would allow. The sails snapped above me, and the timber of the boat creaked. We were already racing at top speed.

"Lose some weight," my sister snapped without turning.

She didn't mean *my* weight, but for a second I couldn't help thinking that she did. My big bones were usually on my mind.

Waulnk!

The necrowhal rammed the ice again. This time the vibration rattled my teeth.

"Noah, help me!" Ian barked. His voice was strained and less human than ever. It rumbled up from deep in his throat.

The sound of it worried me almost as much as the

necrowhal. Naomi and I knew little about Ian, and even less about werewolves. By agreeing to help him, we could have gotten ourselves into bigger trouble than we imagined.

"Hurry," he added, seeing me pause.

I shook off my fears and scampered to his side. Now wasn't the time to hesitate. No matter what secrets Ian kept, he wanted to escape the necrowhal as much as I did.

I would just have to keep an eye on him once we were safe.

Together we struggled to untie the boat's anchor. Ian had hauled it over the railing by himself. He was stronger than I'd realized. Not even my father could lift the anchor alone.

When the last frozen knot came undone, I exhaled loudly. My fingers were raw and ached with cold, so I stuck them under my armpits.

"Can you get it?" I asked Ian quickly.

He nodded beneath his hood. Then he scooped up the anchor and pitched it over the rear of the boat. I actually felt the weight of it drift away.

Unfortunately, so did the necrowhal.

Clarsh! The anchor crashed to the ice.

Waulnk! The necrowhal slammed us again.

The combination was disastrous. Shrieking ice cracked and buckled. Freezing water erupted in geysers, stinging us with bits of ice like needlespine pines.

"Get down!" I yelped, dragging Ian to the deck. Sometimes my size came in handy.

Dropping the anchor, I realized, was the worst thing we could have done. Its impact on the ice had helped the necrowhal break through.

Skree-keek!

Suddenly a piercing screech filled the air. It shattered ice, cracked the railings, and rattled my teeth. Even my eyes watered at the terrible sound.

The necrowhal didn't have eyes. It used its squeal like a bat using radar, by finding and feeling echoes. And right then, the monster was looking for us.

Skree-keek!

Shaped like an overgrown catfish, it was twice the length of our boat. A huge mouth slashed its face like an unhealed wound filled with hooked teeth. The corpse-grey skin of a ghoul covered it from tip to tail.

Some sailors feared sharks, some tidal hydras and serpents. But everyone in Neverthaw feared necrowhals, from South Village to North. In Icefathom Deep, they were as deadly as dragons.

Sharnk! Sharnk!

Tentacles on the monster's sides whipped forward, stretching to amazing lengths like warm taffy. Their razor-sharp tips stabbed the ice as surely as a mountain climber's spikes.

Then the beast pulled itself ahead on its belly. Slithering, squirming, and screeching, it continued to gain on us.

Skree-keek!

"What next?" I shouted up at my sister. Tossing the anchor hadn't worked, but I wasn't ready to give up. Naomi was still our captain and knew the most about sailing.

"I don't know!" she wailed. "Jump off and push!"

That wasn't the leadership I was hoping for, and I knew she wasn't serious. Anyone could tell that. Anyone but Ian, that was.

Arrrr-roooo!

Howling the way he had the night before, he scrambled up and to the edge of the boat.

"What are you doing?" I cried after him. "Stop!" He was really going to jump.

He turned briefly, threw off his hood, and winked at me with one yellow eye. Then he bayed once more and launched himself over the shattered rail.

Skree-keek!

12

"He's crazy!" I shouted to no one. "He's a crazy werewolf!" I couldn't decide which was worse—being crazy or being a werewolf.

Ian had vaulted over the rail and was down on the ice. Down with the necrowhal. Even now he was sprinting toward the monster on all fours.

Arrrr-roooo!

He was crazy, all right. Totally nuts! But so was I, because I was going after him.

Naomi tried to stop me. "I'll turn us around," she offered. "We can sail in close and—"

I cut her off with a wave of my hand.

"No you won't," I said forcefully, trying hard to sound like a big brother. Like someone she would listen to. "Keep your distance until my signal."

Not that I had a signal, really. I just didn't want her

anywhere near the necrowhal. I would figure out how to get her attention later.

Before she could disagree, I turned my back and heaved Stormfall up off the deck. I felt my face go red with strain, and was glad Naomi couldn't see it.

Some big brother, I grumbled to myself. *I can hardly lift my father's hammer.*

From there I stumbled to the rail and toppled over like a chopped tree. Later I would call it a jump or even something more heroic. But deep inside I knew the truth. My going over the rail was a planned fall.

Flomp!

The hammer and I landed with one dull thud. Cracks snaked through the ice beneath us but didn't split wide.

That's a first, I observed. *Something tough enough to hold my big bones without breaking.*

This was, however, no time for gratitude. The necrowhal was bearing down on me like an oncoming avalanche. Its tentacles sprang and slashed forward, stabbing the ice.

Sharnk! Sharnk!

"Ian!" I screamed, scrambling backward.

Now that I was on the ice, I realized that I hadn't thought my plan all the way through. I didn't know the next step. I didn't know what to do!

The necrowhal towered over me like a cresting wave about to fall. Its fanged mouth yawned open. Gooey strands of slobber stretched between its grub-colored lips.

Skree-keek!

Then a blast of solid sound clobbered me. It shot out from blowhole-like vents in the monster's head. Slime splattered me from head to toe.

The necrowhal definitely knew where I was after that one.

"Ian!" I cried again. "Any time now!"

Where is he? I raved silently. A slew of unpleasant possibilities swirled in my mind.

He's gone. The necrowhal swallowed him whole.

He fled. I have the monster's attention, so Ian decided to run.

There wasn't a single hopeful thought among them.

I opened my mouth to scream a third time. The necrowhal wasn't the only one with a big trap. I gulped a breath and—

"Get down!" Ian roared, almost directly into my ear.

I threw myself flat on my back, no questions asked. Werewolf versus necrowhal would be a better fight than big-boned boy versus necrowhal. I just didn't make much of an opponent, especially clutching a hammer I could barely lift.

A snarling brownish blur hurdled over me. It was Ian-to-the-rescue. Maybe my doubts about him were wrong.

He flew straight into the necrowhal's face. Teeth snapped on both sides. Claws flashed and tentacles slashed. I'd never seen such a brutal battle.

"Your hammer!" he barked. Somehow he had managed to scamper onto the necrowhal's back. His cloak was a shredded rag, and his chest heaved for breath. "Break a hole in the ice!"

Astonished, I blinked at him, but caught on quick. Break the ice and force the monster back underwater. Why hadn't I thought of it? The plan was so simple.

Because it's hopeless, I knew. A hole would drag Ian and me into the water, too. We would drown, freeze, or be swallowed. What choices!

I hesitated for only a moment before deciding. Then I grasped Stormfall with both hands and started to heave. I was going to get the hammer over my head if it was the last thing I ever did.

Almost

13

Almost.

That single word was my battle cry. I repeated it, clung to it, and it gave me strength. I could lift my father's hammer, I knew I could. I was almost there.

At the moment, Stormfall rested heavily on my shoulder. My legs shook beneath its weight. My arms burned with strain. But I had never lifted the hammer so high before.

Almost, Noah. Almost.

If I'd had the breath, I would have shouted the word. *Almost!*

"Hurry, Noah!" Ian roared. Apparently he had lots of breath. What he didn't have was time.

In a glance, I saw the necrowhal buck like a wild stallion and send him flying. The fight between them ended faster than it had begun.

Arrrr-roooo! Ungh!

Ian crash-landed at my feet a blink later. New splinters cracked the ice.

"Now!" he rasped at me in obvious pain. He had given his all and was letting me know that it was my turn. "Break the ice!"

I grunted, heaving upward again. *Al-l-l-l-most.*

Then suddenly, Stormfall was above me. My elbows lurched up to my temples, and the hammer teetered over my head.

"Finally!" I cried. Almost was over. What a day! What a victory! Everything was brand new.

Lifting Stormfall meant so much. Mostly that my muscles had caught up to my weight. I wasn't just a chubby kid anymore. Today big-boned meant big-muscled too.

"Hey, Naomi, loo—!" I started to shout. I was so thrilled that I momentarily forgot Ian, the ice, and the necrowhal.

Skree-keek!

But the monster hadn't forgotten. Its piercing screech struck me dead on. Icy air and the stench of dead fish blasted me. Then its tentacles snapped forward.

Sharnk! Sharnk!

They stabbed into the ice and sent tremors rumbling beneath my feet. One moment I was standing proud, arms raised and hammer high. The next I was falling backward as woodenly as a toy soldier. I might as well have been frozen.

I didn't have time to scream or cry out. I doubt I even blinked. The fall took me by surprise and the landing broke my heart.

Whoolmp!

I crashed flat onto my back, and the hammer slipped uselessly from my hands.

What a failure!

That was my new cry. It was in my head. That was me. I was a big-boned failure. Never had I felt worse.

Stormfall was still too much for me. I couldn't really lift it, not when it mattered. My *almost* wasn't nearly good enough.

What a failure.

As I lay there on the ice, the necrowhal wriggled closer. Its bloated body was almost on top of us. Its pale skin glistened like the fat on a strip of bacon.

What a way to go, I thought dryly. *Gobbled up by the one thing that's fatter than me.*

I tried to roll over and run. That's what failures did. They ran from trouble and danger instead of facing them.

C-r-r-r-renck!

But in that instant, the whole world started to tilt and grind. Huge slabs of ice tipped into the sea like sinking ships. The grey sky spun overhead, and water rushed into my ears.

We're going to drown, I panicked, shivering with terror. *Stormfall has broken the ice, and we're all going to drown.*

And that was it. Stormfall really had broken the ice. My dropping it was enough to shatter the ice around us.

What power! I marveled. *From an accidental drop!* How I wished I could use it. The hammer was mightier than I had ever imagined.

C-r-r-r-renck!

It was also more dangerous, I realized too late. That one drop had doomed us all. The icy sea was going to swallow us whole.

On the Menu

14

"Noah, my hand!" someone shouted nearby.

The voice sounded familiar, but I could barely make out the words. Freezing water sloshed in my ears. Ice groaned all around.

"*N*-Naomi?" I gasped weakly. She was the person I most wanted to see, and the one I least wanted to be here. I had hoped she was safe and far away. I had also hoped she was coming to rescue me.

A furry hand gripped mine and started to pull. It wasn't Naomi's. It was Ian's.

"The hammer!" I blurted. Losing it in the sea would be unthinkable. I could never explain that to my father.

"Got it," the werewolf growled. "Now hang on!"

Ian was strong. I've mentioned that. In one hand—one *paw*—he clutched Stormfall. With the other he dragged me out of the water and onto a tipsy slab of ice.

"Here," he huffed, passing the hammer to me. "I can hardly lift it."

Hearing that almost made me laugh. A werewolf with superhuman strength could hardly lift the hammer? Think about me! My failure to lift it had nearly drowned us.

As it was, we weren't safe yet. We were floating in the middle of a frozen sea. Drowning was a deadly possibility.

Sharnk! Sharnk!

One of many.

Suddenly one of the necrowhal's tentacles knifed up through the ice. The monster was directly beneath us! It had slithered into the water and was attacking from below.

Sharnk! Sharnk!

Again and again its tentacles pierced the ice and lanced into the air. First to our left, then right, slashing ever closer.

"Keep moving!" Ian barked in warning. He was on all fours and scampering lightly across the ice. "Stay on your toes!"

Easy for you to say, I wanted to snap. *Look at how many toes you have.* Ian's wolfish hands could double as paws whenever he wanted.

Still I did my best to follow his lead. I lumbered one way and then the next. A moving target was harder to hit, even a big-boned one.

Sharnk! A tentacle sliced up inches away from my face. *Sharnk!* The second brushed my cloak.

"Not that way!" Ian yipped, seeing me in danger.

I made a face at him. "Like that helps!" I snapped. We never knew where the necrowhal would strike next.

Sharnk! Sharnk! But it always seemed to know exactly where we were going.

Next the tentacles stabbed diagonally through the ice like crossed swords. Ian dropped onto his shaggy belly and slid beneath them an instant before an awful collision.

"Hot dog!" I couldn't resist shouting. Get it? Were*wolf*. Hot *dog*. His narrow escape reminded me of a daring acrobat showing off for a crowd.

"Better than a scaredy cat," he shot back. He grinned his werewolf's grin as he said it. Tongue out, lips curled up at the corners.

"Oh, go chase your tail!" Naomi chimed in unexpectedly.

Still aboard the outrigger, she coasted up alongside our slab of ice. A channel of churning water separated her from us, but I'd never been happier to hear her mouth.

"That's telling him!" I cheered. I could always count on her to stick up for me. Now I could count on her for a ride out too.

"What makes you think I was talking to him?" she responded.

Sisters! I should have known.

"Just get us out of here!"

Sharnk! Sharnk!

The necrowhal attacked again. While the rest of us were making jokes, it was still thinking about dinner.

And guess who was on the menu.

"Noah!" Naomi shrieked.

That's right. Big-boned me was the main course.

Without warning, the monster changed its strategy. Instead of attacking from below, it came at us head-on again.

First its tentacles stabbed the ice, chopping downward like falling axes. Then it heaved its immense bulk out of the water and onto the slab.

Flaumphff!

What a belly smacker! The monster landed half in and half out of the sea. When it hit the ice, the slab tilted, and we started to slide.

Ian howled and his nails scratched uselessly on the slippery ice. I screamed, clutching Stormfall with both hands.

Nothing helped. We were sliding headfirst toward the necrowhal, and there was nothing between us and its waiting open mouth.

Boatering Ram

15

Teeth, bared lips, and a gooey tongue as big as a mattress filled my vision. The necrowhal waited below the way dogs wait for table scraps—drooling and ready to pounce. It was only a matter of time.

Ian and I slipped helplessly closer to the gaping maw. We couldn't hang on. The slab of ice beneath us was too slick and its angle too steep. All the monster needed to do was wait.

Skree-keek!

It shrieked once, confident but impatient. How long it had hunted us!

Not that I minded the hunt. I was all for it. The longer it lasted, the longer the necrowhal went without dinner.

"Naomi is trouble," Ian growled suddenly. It was an odd thing to say and an odd time to say it, and just a bit rude.

"What's that supposed to mean?" I snapped at him. It

wasn't her fault that we were about to be eaten. We were on Ian's quest.

"It means *jump*!" he howled, and then he did just that. He sprang straight into the air from all fours like a startled cat. Just don't tell him I said that.

I jumped too. At least I tried. I wasn't a werewolf or even a cat, but the look on Ian's face told me to jump, and fast.

"Ungh!"

Maybe most of me made it into the air, maybe not. Either way, the jump got my big bones moving just in time.

Because right then Naomi sailed straight into the necrowhal.

Splooom!

It was the craziest stunt I'd ever seen. She didn't turn at the last moment, and she didn't slow down. The outrigger was a battering ram and the necrowhal a raised castle drawbridge.

"What are you doing?" I bellowed. But my words were lost in the noise and confusion that followed.

Water erupted everywhere. The necrowhal shrieked, our boat creaked, and Ian let out a howl.

I plunged into the cold sea, Stormfall still in my two-fisted grasp. Letting go just wasn't an option. The hammer could not be replaced.

I expected Stormfall to drag me down like an anchor. I imagined a mighty struggle.

Instead an amazing thing happened. We sank for only a moment. The water darkened. Then we started to rise.

Splorsh!

Together we popped up out of the depths like a cork. My lungs heaved for air, but my lips couldn't hold back a smile.

Stormfall could float! Who would have guessed? The hammer that was too heavy to lift could float on water like the lightest leaf.

"It floats!" I cried spontaneously. My shock was too much to contain.

"Imagine that!" Naomi replied, dripping with sarcasm. "A magic hammer that behaves magically. Amazing!"

So much for her always sticking up for me.

"Now quit goofing off and grab on," she added.

Spish!

A rope splashed into the water nearby, and I snatched it eagerly. Then it went taunt as Naomi started to pull on the other end. She was standing on the ice ahead, feet planted and face set in concentration.

How she had gotten there, I could only imagine—a lucky jump over the rail, I guessed. She should have ended up like our boat.

Even now the necrowhal was clutching the boat in its tentacles and squeezing. The monster's angry shrieks and the sound of snapping timber echoed over the sea.

Goodbye, boat, I thought glumly. We had a long walk home when this was over.

Still reeling me in, Naomi chattered idly. "Pretend I'm fishing. With you for bait, how big a fish will I catch?"

I groaned at her through chattering teeth. A big-boned joke! How hysterical.

"*Puh-puh*-please hurry," I stuttered, beginning to feel the cold now that my panic was fading.

Neverthaw parkas were made to repel water and moisture. They kept warm and dry in most conditions. But floating in the middle of the sea was different. There was little protection against that.

"I've got it!" Naomi beamed, seeming to ignore my request. "I would probably catch that dogfish over there."

She meant Ian, who was swimming toward us. He looked as miserable as I felt, almost sickly skinny with wet fur plastered to his body. Doing the doggy paddle didn't help his appearance.

"Or is it a wolf-fish?" Naomi smirked. "A werefish?"

Her mouth was working double-time today. Normally that could mean trouble, but she had saved us from the necrowhal. We could forgive her yapping.

"You're in for it," Ian snarled. Then again, maybe he wasn't the forgiving type.

When he reached the ice, Ian scrambled out of the water, planted his feet, and shook from head to toe to tail. Naomi squealed and raised her hands, but she couldn't avoid a thorough soaking.

"Can a werefish do that?" Ian taunted playfully. "Or a

dogfish?"

Splook!

Suddenly a snowball struck him on the nose, and he snapped his mouth shut and blinked. Naomi fell over, howling with laughter. Both of them had their eyes on me.

I shrugged and spread my arms, trying to look innocent. It didn't work. Naomi and Ian knew that I had thrown the snowball, and they were after me as soon as their surprise wore off.

"No, no!" I protested, starting to run. "It was an accident!"

Splook! Splook! Splook!

I didn't get far. Snowballs splattered my back, legs, shoulders, and head. Their aim was uncanny, and my run to freedom quickly turned into handfuls of snow down the back.

"Freezing!" I howled, tearing off my parka and shaking like Ian as best I could. Naomi dropped her snowballs and pointed. Ian stood up on two legs.

"I know, I know," I said, expecting a comment from Naomi. "I look like I'm doing some weird snowman dance, right?"

She shook her head and pointed more urgently. Ian pointed too.

"We're there," he whispered.

I turned, not knowing what to expect. We were there *where?*

As soon as I saw what they were pointing at, I knew. I quit shaking and stared ahead, letting my parka dangle in the snow.

A lone mountain rose up before us like a giant icy stalagmite. Dark crevices burrowed into its depths. Twisting spires and jagged rock formations sprouted from its surface like crooked claws.

What an awful place. Every ounce of me wanted to turn and flee. And that's a lot of ounces.

"Bargain Mountain," Naomi breathed, almost too quietly to be heard.

Ian and I simply nodded. There was nothing else to say. We were standing on the doorstep of a dragon.

Bargain Mountain Climbing

16

Even Naomi kept quiet as the three of us gazed up at Bargain Mountain. We squinted against the light reflecting off its sharp angles and stared with our mouths open.

The frozen mountain paid no attention to us in return. It reached silently into the sky, unaware of our presence, or unimpressed.

Which was exactly how I wanted it. We didn't need the mountain giving us trouble. The dragon would be trouble enough.

Hungry trouble, I added. Dragons were known for many things, including their appetites. We would be just a snack.

I hoped Ian appreciated what we were doing.

As if he could hear my thoughts, he interrupted our silent study of the mountain.

"Please wait for me here," he said softly, eyes never straying from the dragon's lair. "I'll try to hurry." With that, he dropped to all fours and prepared to run.

Naomi stopped him with a hand on his shoulder.

"No," she told him. "We go together. The three of us. We're a team."

I nodded in solemn agreement. Of course my first thought was to turn immediately and run home. The dragon would probably be the death of us.

Deep inside, however, I knew that helping Ian was the right thing to do. He needed us. Being trapped in a werewolf's body and not knowing who he was must have been terrifying. We couldn't abandon him.

"That's right," I agreed. "Not so fast. Some of us have to drag big hammers up that mountain." Lucky me, the entrance was a cavern near the peak. It would be a long climb with Stormfall on my belt.

Ian peered briefly over his shoulder at us, and his tongue lolled out. He flashed a smile.

"Thank you," he said. Then he turned rapidly and started bounding toward the mountain.

I couldn't be sure, but the fur on his cheeks might have reddened. The sight left me wondering whether werewolves could blush.

The trek up Bargain Mountain was hard, and Stormfall didn't make it any easier. The hammer had been nothing but a heavy piece of luggage on this quest. How I wished I could carry it normally!

We climbed a steep trail that wound around the

mountainside like the chambers in a snail's shell. The trail was wide enough for a wagon and horses, but so icy that we were forced to crawl in spots.

Only Ian had little trouble. He switched between two and four legs often, and his claws could usually get a good grip. He used his werewolf's advantages as if he had been using them his whole life. He was certainly getting used to his new body.

"Why do mountains have to be so tall?" I panted as we took a short rest. We were halfway up and all the way exhausted.

Ian sniffed the ice and his ears drooped.

"Good question," he replied. "But this mountain isn't natural. Someone or some*thing* built it."

Hearing that, I stood quickly. I wanted as little as possible of me touching the mountain. The bottoms of my boots were more than I liked.

"Not natural—how?" I asked, my voice cracking a little.

"Do you mean it's magic?" Naomi interjected. Her eyes widened with excitement.

Ian didn't respond immediately. He padded here and there, pausing to sniff things I couldn't see. Finally he sat down across from us.

"I don't know," he confessed. "A dragon lives here, that's for sure. Her scent clings to everything—the snow and ice, the rocks, even us."

He paused and Naomi piped up eagerly. "But?"

The werewolf nodded. "But other things live here too. Cold things. Thousands of them. They burrow through the mountain like … like maggots in the trash."

"Gross!" Naomi exclaimed. "You look like a werewolf, but you're all boy. Gross, gross, gross!" She climbed to her feet. "I'm going up. Are you *boys* coming with me?"

Ian and I looked helplessly at each other and shrugged. There was no telling what would start Naomi's mouth running. It was best to just go along with her.

"Coming!" he and I chimed together.

The second half of our climb left us breathless and sweating. Even Ian's head sagged and his chest heaved when we finally reached the top.

"Are we there yet?" I whined like an impatient kid on a long trip.

"Don't make me turn this outrigger around," Naomi responded in a deep voice. She said it the way our father would, and had. I was too tired to grin.

A dark cavern mouth full of stalactites like icy fangs yawned before us. The stalactites gave the cavern a hungry look.

How many things are going to want to eat us today? I wondered grimly. *First a necrowhal, then a dragon, and now a cavern. What could be next?*

In wondering that, I tried hard not to think about the maggots Ian had sensed.

But the unpleasant thought popped into my head, and I

couldn't shake it. Maybe a dragon wasn't the hungriest creature that lived in the mountain.

"Let's get this over with," I said loudly. Anything to get my mind off being eaten.

Naomi reached out and clasped Ian's hand and mine. Her mittens felt surprisingly warm, which was nice right then.

"Here we go," she said, taking the first step into the black cavern.

Icy Ogress Detour

17

Blamp!

"I can't see," I complained. Twenty steps into the cavern and my shins were aching. I had bumped them against who-knows-what half a dozen times already. The cavern was that dark.

Blamp!

"Can anyone else see?"

Naomi shushed me with a hiss.

"Do you want everything to know we're here?" she snapped. "You could light a fire or sing a song."

By *everything*, she meant the dragon and Ian's unnamed maggot-monsters.

So I took a deep breath and got ready to sing. I'd show her what sassy was all about.

To grow up strong
The mountain way,
We lift and press
Big stones all—*Ow!*

Before I finished the verse, Naomi elbowed me in the ribs. Sisters! I hadn't been singing that loudly, only a whisper.

"Here," Ian cut in. "Hold this and follow me. I can see." He handed the edge of his frayed cloak to us.

As he led, we shuffled through the cavern and into a tunnel beyond. Not once more did I bang my shins, and only twice more did Naomi jab me in the ribs.

When a faint glow appeared ahead, I pointed it out gratefully.

"Something's up there," I reported. "I see light."

Ian nodded. "Stay close. The scent of the dragon is strong."

Now that he mentioned it, I realized that I could smell something too. The odor wasn't terrible but it was definitely strong. It reminded me of musty books and leather, like a very old and cluttered library.

Ian stopped suddenly, causing Naomi and me to bump into his back.

"Wolfsbane!" he exclaimed, surprised.

"What?" Naomi demanded. "What is it?" She nimbly scooted past him and then gasped. "How awful!"

Ian moved aside to let me look. My breath caught at the

77

sight, and I winced.

"Is that … was that …?" I bumbled, horrified by what I saw.

"An ogre," Ian confirmed, sniffing the air tentatively. "Well, an ogress actually."

As wide as two adults and almost as tall, the ogress blocked the tunnel. She stood with her meaty hands clenched into fists and one foot in the air like a runner. Her ragged hair was suspended behind her as if blowing in the wind.

The problem was, the wind wasn't blowing. None of us were even breathing. The tunnel was as still as a crypt.

The ogress was frozen in a thick block of ice as though in a transparent cocoon. She couldn't move, breathe, or even blink. Her brutish face depicted total dread and despair.

"I can't look!" Naomi wailed, and hid her face in her hands.

I wanted to do the same, but the ogress' unblinking stare held me. She seemed to be watching me, and I was sure that she was trying to—

"Halp me, leedle peeples."

—speak.

Hearing the words made me flinch as if stuck by a needlespine needle. The ogress had spoken! Her lips hadn't moved. She was trapped under ice. But I heard her beg for help.

"*Sh*-she's alive," I murmured, backing away. "She's

frozen alive!"

I was near panic. My limbs tingled and my heart raced. For once I was sure that lifting Stormfall and running wouldn't be a problem.

"This way," Ian said, taking charge. "There's nothing we can do at the moment. We'll find out what happened to her." Then he crouched low, leaped, and scrambled over the ogress and her block of ice. It was the only route past her.

I swallowed hard and met her weary gaze again.

"We'll come back," I promised. "And we'll find a way to save you." I genuinely meant the words. Not even an ogress deserved to be frozen alive.

The climb wasn't as easy for Naomi and me as it was for Ian. We couldn't jump the way he could, and we didn't have claws. So we tried to scramble over the ice block many times before we finally made it. We spent the whole time apologizing to the ogress.

"Pardon me!" Naomi exclaimed, her knee smacking inches from the ogress' nose.

"'Scuse me," I grunted as my belly mashed against the ice.

"Please forgive my feet."

And Stormfall just made it worse. Dragging the hammer up and over was bumpy business.

"Sorry—"

Clunk!

"—about—"

Clurnk!

"—this."

Clurnk!

Once we were past the ogress, I expected to take a short rest. Unfortunately there wasn't time, and this wasn't the place.

The tunnel entered a huge icy cavern. Light shone in from a wide hole in the ceiling and glinted off dozens of frozen victims entombed in blocks of ice. They stood, cowered, crouched, and knelt throughout the cavern like the sad statues of a lost battle.

There was no mistaking the cavern. We had come to the dragon's lair.

Frozen Alive

18

Erzua's lair was not what I expected. I had imagined piles of gold coins as deep as bathtubs lying on the floor. Magic swords, crowns, suits of armor, and jewels would peek from the shining mounds.

Instead books, scrolls, parchments, and tablets crowded the cavern. Some teetered in leaning stacks. Others filled shelves made of solid ice. Many lay in jumbled heaps, seemingly forgotten.

Talk about an old and cluttered library! We'd found the source of the bookish smell.

Among the books stood rows of blocks of ice like tombstones in a graveyard. Frozen in each was a different captive. In just one glance, I spotted a polar bear, a goblin wearing an eyepatch, a centaur, two river nymphs with spotted skin, and some kind of one-eyed octopus monster. The list could go on and on.

Like the ogress in the tunnel, none of the icy victims moved. They were helpless. But all of them begged to be rescued. Their muffled screams filled my ears.

"Hel-l-l-l-p me!"

"Break da ice!"

"Pleasepleasepleasepleaseplease!"

Listening to them quickly became too much. Any longer and they would drive me insane.

"Now what?" I asked to drown them out. I was almost eager to meet the dragon. Anything but more screams.

"I think we should—" Naomi started.

"STAY AWHILE!" finished a voice like a thundercloud.

This new voice wasn't trapped in ice. It *was* ice—as cold as frost and as sharp as icicles. It made my joints ache and my lungs burn.

It's Erzua! I wanted to shriek. The dragon was here, and she was cold. So cold!

But I couldn't speak, and there was no need. Naomi and Ian knew what I knew. Erzua's presence filled the cavern like ice in a bottle threatening to burst.

She fell on us from overhead, changing color. First clear and smooth, then milky white, then as blue as a shiver. The hole in the ceiling darkened as her color deepened.

She's a chameleon, I realized in awe. *She's been here the whole time, and we couldn't see her. She can blend in with ice and snow.*

Knowing that helped little now. It was too late to run. I

82

All we could do was leap out of her way.

Crish! Crosh! Crash!

Naomi, Ian, and I dove for safety in different directions. Books and scrolls scattered beneath us. Ice and snow crunched and squeaked.

THWO-OO-OOND!

Erzua landed between us, a hammer pummeling an anvil. Ice cracked, snow fell, and tremors rumbled through the ground. For a moment, I feared the whole mountain would collapse.

"I DO SO ENJOY COMPANY!" the dragon bellowed. Her mighty head swung on its serpent's neck to spy the three of us.

Erzua was huge. Her wings blotted out the light, and her bulk crowded the cavern. How something so large could fly bewildered me.

She was part lizard, part bird, part dream and legend. Blue scales like polished glass wrapped her in armor. Fearsome claws and fangs as long as my thighs armed her for war.

Nothing could have prepared me for meeting a dragon up close. Nothing I had imagined could be more deadly.

We're going to die, was my first thought, and likely my last. The dragon was an executioner standing at the gallows.

"Let us talk," she purred, quietly now, like someone in complete control. "We have a deal to make."

nodded stiffly, eager to agree. Doing so might just keep us alive.

"Good, good," she continued, head turning slowly. A wicked smile played at the corners of her mouth, and I assumed that Ian and Naomi were nodding too.

Her smile expanded. "Allow me to ensure your cooperation. The pain will be brief."

Before any of us could scream, she sucked in an enormous breath. The force of it drained the chill from the air, and the temperature in the cavern rose noticeably.

"What's happening?" I gasped.

Wooo-ooo-ooo!

The surprise warmth was temporary. Erzua exhaled loudly, and the cold returned in a shock. It blasted me from head to toe, stinging and burning like icy flames.

We're being frozen alive! I panicked. *Just like the ogress. We'll be trapped in blocks of ice forever!*

A Wealth of Knowledge

19

Roaring like a storm, the dragon's bitter breath blasted my feet and steamed upward. It stung my toes like a thousand needlespine pines, and froze my boots to the ground. In no time I was stuck.

"It's happening!" I wailed, my first thought. The dragon really was freezing me alive.

Strangely I thought of fire next. Not in the hope of warming up but out of curiosity. Dragons were supposed to breathe fire, I'd thought. Was Erzua some kind of mutant?

Long, cold seconds passed as if time itself were freezing. Frost swirled in smoky white clouds. Icy pellets swatted my skin. My world was a howling white blur, and I couldn't see past my fingertips.

Naomi shrieked and Ian yelped, but their voices seemed far away. My own screams sounded muted in my ears as the dragon's breath droned on.

Wooo-ooo-ooo!

And then there was silence. A perfect silence heard only on a winter evening when new snow blankets everything in sight. There were no screams and no gusting air. A gentle quiet cradled all.

The clouds, too, slowly settled, drifting down like ash. They revealed the dragon directly ahead of us, smirking and lounging easily on her belly. She looked quite pleased with herself.

The rest of us weren't so comfortable. We were frozen in place. Blocks of ice entombed our feet and reached almost to our knees. We weren't frozen completely solid like the ogress, but we couldn't get away either.

"What's the big idea?" Naomi demanded angrily. A mittened hand pointed defiantly at the dragon. Even frozen, she was up to her old tricks.

"Shh!" I hissed at her. "Not now." This definitely wasn't the time for her mouth. When was, I didn't know.

Erzua chuckled in response. She arched her long neck and tilted back her head. A sound like cracking glass repeated deep in her throat.

"Such unusual guests," she commented between chuckles.

"Guests?" Naomi nearly shrieked. "*Guests!* This is how you treat company?"

My sister was braver than I'd realized—braver and more foolish. Shouting at a dragon was brave, but it was also a quick way to become lunch.

"Naomi, I mean it," I warned. "Keep your mouth shut."

"Those who arrive uninvited rarely bring friendship," Erzua stated, ignoring me. "We have yet to determine your motivation."

Her words weren't plain, but I grasped their meaning. Erzua didn't trust us, and we had to prove ourselves to her. Otherwise she would consider us intruders.

Fair enough, I tried to accept. We had just sneaked into her home, after all.

Out of the corner of my eye, I saw Naomi bite her lip. She was calming down but not ready to give up.

"But ..." she protested. "We're here to make a deal."

Surprisingly that statement made the dragon laugh harder. Her sides rumbled, freeing bits of snow and ice from her scales. They sparkled briefly in the air like fire-flies before falling. Even a scale or two came loose.

Seeing that made me blink. Was Erzua shedding like a snake?

"Look around you, human," she growled. "Many come to bargain. Few accept the terms."

She meant the frozen prisoners. They had come to make deals, but had failed or refused to pay. Erzua had frozen them as punishment.

"How long will they stay like that?" I blurted, shocking even myself.

The dragon swung her horned head to face me, and her

eyes narrowed.

"One hundred years," she stated flatly. The words were clearly a threat meant for us. She would freeze us, too, if we failed to please her.

I was sorry I'd asked the question.

"You don't scare us," Naomi fired, still defiant. Then she took a deep breath, preparing to say more.

Ian quickly cut her off.

"She means we aren't looking for trouble," he explained. "We don't want a fight, and we're not here to rob you. We have just one question."

"As if there's anything here to steal!" Naomi scoffed. "Just a bunch of old books. Some dragon's treasure this is."

That did it. Naomi's big mouth had enraged the dragon. My sister had really gone to far.

"ENOUGH!" Erzua roared so loudly that the ice around our feet shattered. We could have run if fear hadn't kept us paralyzed.

"You value gold and jewels above books? Above knowledge?" she snarled. "Fools! Knowledge *is* wealth. Such 'old books' are the very source of every power and strength in the world."

She suddenly leaned in close and lowered her head. Her yellow eyes bored into ours, and her cold breath chilled our faces.

"*Carpe draco,* children," she whispered, almost a cat's

purr. "Seize the dragon. Know what we know. Then you will be able to discover your own answers, and you won't need ours."

With that, she spread her velvety wings and leaped into the air. In seconds she vanished from sight, and we were left alone in her frozen lair.

20

Shivering in the cold, we stared anxiously at the hole in the cavern's ceiling. Grey clouds scudded past, but the dragon did not return. We were truly alone.

Whether that was a blessing or curse remained to be seen.

Finally Ian crouched, lifted his face toward the ceiling, and howled.

Arrrr-roooo!

It was one of the saddest sounds I'd ever heard, like weeping in the dead of night. Erzua had been Ian's only hope for breaking his terrible curse and regaining his lost memories.

"Don't worry, Ian," I said lamely. "We'll figure something out."

Saying the words almost embarrassed me. They sounded so unhelpful. But Ian needed reassurance from his friends.

The exact words we used weren't important.

"That's right," Naomi added. "Erzua will be back. She has to come home eventually."

Exactly how long *eventually* might be, we were afraid to wonder. The dragon punished her victims by freezing them for one hundred years. She could obviously wait a long time.

Naomi and I didn't mention this, of course. Instead we patted Ian on the shoulder and tried to cheer him up.

"When she gets back, I'll even keep quiet," Naomi promised. She made a zipping motion across her mouth and ended it by turning and throwing away the key.

Ian stared hard at her for several seconds. He was going to howl again or bite her, I thought. He surprised me by laughing.

"Like that'll ever happen," he snickered, rolling his eyes. "You haven't been quiet since your parents pulled your thumb out of your mouth."

I laughed, too, because it was true. My sister hadn't shut up almost since the day she was born.

Naomi tried to hide her own grin by turning her back on us. The other side of the cavern was suddenly very interesting to her, or so she pretended.

"*Carpe draco,*" she chided us, using the dragon's words. "*Carpe draco,* boys."

Now it was my turn to stare. Ian hadn't stopped.

"What's that supposed to mean?" he and I demanded

together.

Naomi turned, no longer hiding her grin. She looked as smug as Erzua had while resting on her belly.

"It means whatever you want it to mean," Naomi shrugged. "Be the best. Achieve. Succeed. Do something important. You get it?"

She could tell by our clueless looks that we didn't, so she tried again. First she faced Ian.

"You want to break your curse, right?" she said, not really a question.

He nodded, grimacing slightly.

"Then do it. *Carpe draco!*"

Without pausing, she turned to me. "And you want to carry daddy's hammer, not just drag it around."

Like Ian, I nodded.

"Then try until you can," she beamed. "Never give up. *Carpe draco!*"

I was starting to get the idea, but her bubbly superiority annoyed me.

"What if I want Erzua to come back right this very second?" I challenged. "*Carpe—!*"

I never finished. The dragon did that for me.

"*—draco,*" Erzua hissed like winter wind blowing down the chimney.

I froze. "She's right behind me, isn't she?" I asked unnecessarily.

Ian and Naomi nodded, both grinning bashfully. We'd

forgotten about the dragon's ability to camouflage herself. She'd sneaked up on us after vanishing. Who knew how long she'd been listening?

"*Carpe draco* indeed," she agreed. "Now let us see if we cannot strike a deal. My home is called Bargain Mountain for a reason."

The Deal

21

Erzua's deal wasn't much of a deal. She spoke, we listened, and then we had to decide. It was either agree to her terms or leave.

"Find my missing egg," she instructed. "Bring it safely to me, and then I will answer the werewolf's question."

That was it, our deal. Egg first, question later. The order and terms weren't open for discussion.

"We agree," I said without delay. "We'll do it."

I smiled supportively at Ian. Of course we would accept the deal. We had come to get an answer and wouldn't leave until we got one.

"Just, uh, tell us where to look for the egg," I added less confidently.

Erzua ignored me for the moment. She reared suddenly and roared. One claw slammed the frozen ground like a judge striking the gavel to pass sentence.

"So be it!" she bellowed. "The deal is struck and the covenant forged. We are in agreement. Let the terms be met or the punishment served."

Her booming voice echoed a long time before quiet returned to the cavern. When the echoes faded, I realized that I'd been holding my breath. So had Naomi and Ian.

"Be at ease," Erzua smiled, noticing our looks. "Breathe. We are allies now and for the duration of our pact. You have nothing to fear."

Somehow I doubted that. Erzua hadn't told us where her missing egg was yet. There had to be a reason she was keeping that a secret.

"The egg?" Ian prompted her. "Where is it?"

A dark look crossed the dragon's face, and for a moment, she seemed ready to attack. Her eyes blazed fiercely. Her scales glowed like metal heated in a forge. Then the look passed as quickly as it had come.

"The egg is below," she said quietly. "In the clutches of the filthy dracopedes."

Immediately I thought of Ian's unnamed burrowers. He had compared them to maggots. Without doubt, I was sure they were the dracopedes Erzua was talking about.

Knowing that made me shiver. Chasing maggots beneath a dragon's mountain wasn't the kind of egg-hunt I enjoyed.

"Do you have something to put the egg in?" Naomi asked calmly. She hadn't said anything else since the dragon's return. "So it doesn't break."

Erzua's eyes narrowed, regarding my sister coolly. Then the dragon shook her head.

"Unnecessary," she replied. "The egg will not break. But your frail human strength may not bear it." Her eyes shot to me. "Step forward."

I did so slowly, noisily dragging Stormfall behind me. The head of the hammer scraped a channel in the ice like a stick in the dirt.

"Stop," Erzua ordered after I'd taken just a few steps. "That hammer. Is it yours?"

I glanced sheepishly at Stormfall. Wasn't it obvious? No, the hammer wasn't mine. I couldn't even lift it!

Never had I felt weaker or smaller. I was big-boned, yes, even chubby. But that didn't make me strong enough to properly lift my father's hammer. Why had I even brought it along?

"No," I whispered. "The hammer isn't mine. I can't even—"

"Leave him alone!" Naomi cut in, dashing forward and grabbing my arm. Her timing was predictable. Baby sister to the rescue. How embarrassing!

"Now I see it," the dragon mused. "Brother and sister. Very well. You will share the responsibility."

Before we could question what she meant, Erzua sucked in a deep breath. I expected a blast of ice and snow to follow. This time, however, their pain was brief and very well-aimed.

I was struck on the bicep of my left arm, Naomi in the palms of her open hands. Both of us winced at the chilly sensation, then we gasped at what appeared.

An icy blue band like the dragon's scales encircled my upper arm. It pulsed slowly with mysterious light and sent wave after wave of warmth into my skin.

"*H*-how?" I murmured. The band was made of ice yet it felt so warm.

"It's beautiful!" Naomi gaped. "But what do I do with it?"

At first I thought she meant the band on my arm. Then I saw the object in her hands.

It was a crystal yo-yo that looked like two snowflake-shaped sugar cookies pressed together. A delicate strand of silver silk wound around its center and dangled out between its halves.

"Use that to summon my breath," Erzua answered. "But you may do so only with a rhyme. Put that mouth of yours to good use."

Erzua's last comment made me smirk. The dragon had given my sister a gift that would teach her a lesson. Think before you speak.

"And you," the dragon growled, eyes on me again. "Lift the hammer. Now."

Her tone demanded obedience. So I grasped Stormfall in both hands, bent my knees, took a breath, and—

Easily lifted it over my head!

The hammer felt like a balloon, and I like a hero. Stormfall was over my head! What a moment! How I wished my father could see, and that bully Bart.

"How?" I repeated, dumbfounded. My greatest wish had been granted.

"*Carpe draco,*" the dragon responded. "Today you can be great."

Correction, I thought. *Today I am great.* There was no *can be* about it.

"Bring on the dracopedes," I said confidently. I really thought I was ready for them.

22

Soon after leaving Erzua we were shuffling through a rough tunnel. Its low ceiling forced us to stoop often, and sharp ice formations required that we watch our elbows. The three of us were as bruised as mishandled bananas in no time.

There was no way Erzua could squeeze into the narrow tunnel. That explained why she had demanded that we find her missing egg. She couldn't do it herself.

"How far do we have to go?" Naomi wondered.

Ian paused to sniff the air. He was in the lead, Naomi in the middle, and I in the back.

That was fine with me. Front, back, upside down, or sideways didn't matter. With Stormfall in my hands, everywhere was the top of the world.

"Keep your eyes open," Ian warned. "We're getting closer. Their scent is strong."

He meant the scent of the dracopedes. They lurked ahead, scuttling and slinking somewhere in the icy mountain. There were hundreds of them, maybe thousands. One for every scale Erzua had shed.

My eyes hadn't been fooling me when I'd seen the dragon lose a scale. She had, and it hadn't been the first time. She lost them regularly the way a person loses hair during a good brushing. It was normal.

The unusual part was what happened next. Erzua had explained it to us. The scale, the ice, and her magic combined to create nasty critters called dracopedes. They were part dragon, part insect, and all magic.

Dracopedes looked like milky white centipedes and acted a lot like meat-eaters. They were the size of living room sofas, and had stolen Erzua's egg. Somehow we had to defeat them to get it back.

"There!" Ian hissed. "Did you hear that?"

All three of us froze, straining to hear what the werewolf had. We didn't have to listen long.

Krickitic-clack!

The sound came again, a scratching, scraping noise. It tickled our ears and caused our eyes to twitch. The dracopedes were on the move.

"This way," Ian barked, breaking into a four-legged run. "There's an opening ahead. We don't want to get cornered in this tunnel."

On his heels, we scampered into an empty cavern. Dozens of similar tunnels emptied into the place. The walls looked like the surface of the moon.

"Now where?" Naomi asked, spinning as she spoke.

One tunnel looked the same as any other to us—icy, uninviting, and deadly. None of them promised a safe or sure path to the dragon's egg.

I squinted, concentrating hard. Was that movement up ahead? Were the dracopedes to my right? My left?

Klackatac-crick!

Sure enough, I saw them scuttling down the tunnels like ants in a hill. Their legs clacked and their antennae bobbed. In seconds they would swarm us.

"Wolfsbane!" Ian swore. "There's too many to count!"

I glanced at my feet, still squinting, still searching. My eyes spotted something that offered hope, and I formed a fast plan.

"Hang on!" I shouted. Then I raised Stormfall and prepared to swing it down with all my might.

Hammer Time

23

"Hurry!" Ian howled.

"They're coming!" Naomi added.

My friends were trying to help, but their warnings weren't necessary. I saw the dracopedes and heard the clicking of their limbs. The beasts spilled out of the tunnels like slop from a farmer's bucket at feeding time.

Krickitic-clack!

The sound of their charge made my skin crawl, and I wanted to scrub myself as if I'd walked through a spider web.

People often feared creepy critters. Some were afraid of snakes or spiders. Others, like Naomi, hated roaches and the slippery things under rocks. The dracopedes were horrible enough to make everyone shudder.

They were the biggest, ugliest, creepiest insects I'd ever seen. Imagine icy centipedes the size of crocodiles. Cover them in dragon scales and give them pincers. Then pray that they never, ever come for you.

Ian was right in calling them maggots. Maggots were horrible and so were the dracopedes. Thousands rushed us, and more kept coming. They were an army without end.

"Now, Noah!" Naomi cried. "Do it!"

"*Carpe draco!*" I responded, heaving Stormfall downward between my feet.

The hammer descended swiftly, eagerly. It longed for battle, I could tell. Stormfall wanted to smash, to crush, and to flatten and bring the winds.

And with it in my hands, I wanted those things too.

Thwoolm!

When its mighty head slammed the ice, the cavern erupted in white and wind. Lightning flashed, thunder groaned, and the floor beneath us melted away.

We fell, spinning and snowblind. Ian howled, or it could have been the wind. Raging white flooded my vision— pieces of dracopedes, snow, and ice.

Can people drown on dry land? I wondered dreamily. So much was happening and all of it cold. I was afraid of losing myself in the storm.

Blarmmm!

Landing changed that. My back slammed onto the ice, and the air burst from my lungs. I grunted once, no longer afraid. The pain was worse than my fear.

Some plan! I snarled to myself. *Next time think it*

through.

But there hadn't been time for thinking or plans. The dracopedes had charged, and I had acted. It had been that or be trampled by the icy brutes.

What my friends hadn't known was that there was another cavern beneath us. I had spotted it through a narrow crevice in the ice. Our floor was its ceiling, like the second story of a building. So I'd used Stormfall to get us down in a hurry.

It had worked better than I'd imagined.

Faster, too, and more painful.

"Everyone all right?" I groaned, unsure as to whether I was all right myself.

Naomi was the first to respond. I shouldn't have expected anything else.

"Next time a warning would be nice," she sassed. "You blew up all the dracopedes and almost took us with them."

I scrunched up my face. "You told me to swing," I retorted.

She shrugged and gave a toss of her braids. "Since when do you listen to me?"

My jaw dropped, but I couldn't think of anything to say.

Ian finally scrambled out from under the snow, muttering to himself. He paused to shake his fur dry, then met my gaze.

"We're not alone," he said.

He barely got the words out before Naomi shrieked.

"There's more of them!" she wailed.

Turns out Stormfall hadn't blown up all the dracopedes. Many had survived. They were digging themselves out of the rubble and getting ready for a second charge.

Hungry Living Weapons

24

"Consider yourself warned," I told my sister in a hurry. "No surprises this time."

I winked as I raised Stormfall over my head. She scowled but got my point. There would be no grumbling from her later.

"Hmpfh!" she grunted, turning her back to me.

Unfortunately, it didn't matter which way she faced. Dracopedes were scuttling toward us from every direction. Pick one and there was a monster straight ahead.

"Stay close!" Ian barked. "Stand back to back."

He really meant back to back *to back*. There were three of us. So we scooted in tight until our shoulders were almost touching. Then we met the dracopedes' charge.

They advanced with their antennae lowered like knights' lances. Their pincers snapped. Their toothy mouths gaped. The dracopedes were living weapons. *Hungry* living weapons.

The first one to reach us reared up in front of Naomi. Its body creaked like splintering ice as it swatted at her with dozens of its cold legs.

She dodged desperately, her right hand thrown out for balance. From her left hand spun Erzua's yo-yo.

How she had taken off her mittens so quickly amazed me. She was a magician at pulling them off and putting them back on.

"Here goes nothing!" she cried.

Watching her was almost comical. Never had I imagined her going into battle armed with a yo-yo. Just the thought seemed so far-fetched.

About as far-fetched as me lifting Stormfall, I corrected immediately.

Erzua's magic was capable of mighty feats, I realized. The band on my arm was proof of that. I was super strong. Naomi had a magic yo-yo. Sometimes the truth really was as wild as fiction.

My sister feinted right, rolled left, and then came to a stop on her knees. She flicked her wrist and sent the yo-yo streaking into the nearest dracopede.

"Bull's-eye!" I cheered, proud of her.

But the blow had no effect. The yo-yo bounced harm-lessly against the dracopede, and then coiled back into my sister's palm. There was no explosion of ice or flash of magic. The yo-yo seemed as ordinary as any other.

I sighed in disappointment. Naomi had said it. *Here goes nothing*. And that was exactly what she got. Nothing but an angry dracopede.

Enraged, the beast attacked, and Naomi knelt helplessly in front of it. Only Ian's bravery saved her.

Arrrr-roooo!

As I'd see him do before, he leaped into the monster like a wrestler. He was a blur of fur, yelping and snarling.

"The rhyme!" he growled. "You forgot the rhyme!"

His words were for Naomi, not me, but they explained a lot. Erzua had said the yo-yo would only work with a rhyme. *Put that mouth of yours to good use,* she had told my sister.

"Got it!" Naomi shouted. "Thinking!"

I balked. *Thinking?*

Any other time, I probably would have snapped at her. Since when had she ever had trouble coming up with something to say? But with monsters closing in, I could bite my tongue. Now wasn't the easiest time for thinking.

Klackatac-crick!

As it was, two dracopedes attacked me at the same time. They approached from my right and left, charging forward in a deadly V-shaped wedge.

I was caught between them, flat-footed and unprepared. Big-boned me was a big-boned target again. The dracopedes were going to run right over me.

So I did the only thing I could. I let them. But first I

109

tapped Stormfall's handle on the ground in front of me.

Thimp!

Just a light touch was all it took. The result was perfect.

Skrack!

Perfect and loud.

The ice beneath me groaned, and a narrow crevice as deep as a grave split opened at my feet. Without looking, I held my breath and jumped down. The dracopedes raced over me a second later.

Talk about a narrow escape! I had never moved so fast. Stormfall and the dragon's magic were making a hero of me. *Carpe draco* hooray!

As soon as the dracopedes passed, I scrambled out of the crevice. I couldn't turn my quick escape into a disappearing act.

Above, Naomi was chanting and spinning her yo-yo again. As it twirled, it hummed and spat icy sparks into the air. Silver threads like miniature lightning bolts blinked in its wake.

Something magical was about to happen, but what?

Lopsided Battle

25

Still dodging dracopedes, Naomi chanted:

Dragon's breath
Need not be fire.
Feel its chill,
A frozen pyre.

With every word, the yo-yo on her finger spun faster. More and more sparks leaped into the air around it.

"Better do something quick," I said nervously. "That thing sounds like it's going to explode."

The yo-yo whirred shrilly like a boiling kettle. It was a sound of approaching danger, even a warning. I sure hoped my sister knew what she was doing.

She did, or she was good at faking it. With a wink at me, she flicked her wrist and sent the yo-yo flying.

Sku-ooo!

Squealing, it sped from her hand in a straight line. Not even the string slowed it down. The yo-yo snapped its line like the one that got away and kept racing.

"It's loose!" I cried, thinking of a wild animal that had escaped its leash. Where would the yo-yo go next?

Floo-oo-oom!

Straight into a dracopede, that was where. It struck one between the eyes with a solid *crack*. An instant later, the monster exploded into a million tiny pieces.

The yo-yo, however, was unharmed. It zoomed back to Naomi's hand with a fiery silver tail blazing behind it. Then it reattached itself to its string as if nothing had happened.

"Outstanding!" I cheered. The yo-yo really was a weapon, and the dracopedes were just snowmen shaped like monsters. They were ice and old scales, not living creatures.

Knowing that made me comfortable with what happened next. Because we defeated the dracopedes as if we were giants and they children. The fight was hardly fair.

Ian led our counterattack. He darted among the monsters, clawing here and biting there. His yelps and snarls resounded with victory.

Naomi made things easy for him. She flipped her yo-yo one way and then the next. Each toss froze or shattered another dracopede.

As for me, I could have relaxed and watched the excitement. Naomi and Ian were amazing, and the dracopedes didn't stand a chance. My swinging Stormfall just made the battle more lopsided.

Thwoolm! I blasted one into glimmering fragments. *Thwoolm!* Another collapsed in a heap of powdery snow. *Thwoolm! Thwoolm!*

"We're all outstanding!" I roared, feeling superhuman. No ice was too thick, no dracopede too strong. Stormfall and I could defeat them all.

In a break in the action, I spun right then left, looking for more enemies. The hammer pulsed eagerly in my hands. It felt alive, and so did I.

Then I spotted something ahead. Something half-buried and peeking from the ice. It was large, blue, and not moving at all.

A frozen dracopede, I decided quickly. Naomi's yo-yo had struck again.

In three giant steps, I stood before it. Still the thing didn't move. Nevertheless I raised Stormfall, preparing to crush. Naomi stopped me just in time.

"*Nooo!*" she shrieked. "Stop! Stop! That's Erzua's egg. Stop!"

I froze instantly, and Stormfall slipped from my suddenly cold fingers. It fell harmlessly to the ice behind me, landing with a noisy crunch.

The only sound after that was my ragged breathing. I had almost crushed the dragon's icy blue egg.

Chicken Lizard

26

Erzua's egg was the size of a pirate's treasure chest and had a lumpy shell made of cloudy blue ice. I could see inside it as if I were looking at an icicle.

And what I saw there stunned me. A baby dragon lay curled up like a kitten dozing in a patch of sunshine. It was as big as a heron and had pale, soft-looking scales. Their color reminded me of an uncooked chicken.

As I stared, the baby dragon stared back and slowly blinked.

I stumbled backward. "There's a dragon in there," I gasped. "And it … it's awake."

Behind me, Naomi snorted. She probably rolled her eyes too.

"What did you expect, an omelet?" she quipped.

I made a face and crossed my eyes. Sometimes I really wanted to yank those braids on her head.

"I prefer sunny-side up," I fired back. "Hold the lizard." Dragon, lizard—whatever.

We laughed uneasily, more nervous than we wanted to admit. The baby dragon continued to stare. Blink, blink. How I wished the egg had a solid shell!

"Let's test that band on your arm, Noah" Ian suggested. "See if you can lift the egg."

On the outside, I nodded and stepped toward the egg. Inside, I shuddered with disgust. The last thing I wanted to do was to bear-hug a chicken-skinned dragon.

Doing so would give a whole new meaning to *carpe draco*, seize the dragon. The words wouldn't be an idea anymore. They would be me actually cuddling the dragon like a baby doll.

"Let's get this over with," I grunted, wrapping my arms around the egg and starting to tug. The position put me face-to-face with the dragon, and our eyes met briefly. The creature blinked again, and I quickly looked away.

"Chicken lizard," I muttered.

Crrrk ... Crrrk ...

The egg came loose grudgingly, creaking in its icy bed. The thing hadn't been moved in a long time and was frozen to the ground like a sled left out in an ice storm.

Crrrk ... Crrrk ... CRECK-K-K!

When it popped free, the force of it threw me backward. The egg landed on me, and I landed on my back. Any harder and I really would have had an omelet.

They were there when I looked up again. The dragon's big wet eyes. They blinked blankly, impossible to read.

"Oh, stop it!" I snapped. *Opened or closed, just pick one!* The slow-motion blinking was driving me nuts.

Ian and Naomi rolled the egg off my chest, and I leaned gratefully against it. *Blink at the back,* I thought darkly. It was a small victory, but a good one.

"Come on," Naomi said before I caught my breath. "Let's go finish our part of the deal."

I glanced at her and then overhead. The hole in the ceiling was a long way up. Returning to Erzua's lair wasn't going to be easy. How would we get back up?

Naomi noticed my concern and chuckled. "I have a plan," she said, and her eyes sparkled too much for my liking. The look was dangerous.

"More yo-yo tricks?" I guessed.

Her eyes sparkled brighter. "Yep," she agreed. "More yo-yo tricks. Now stand close. We're going for a ride."

Sleeping the Yo-Yo

27

Flashing a grin, Naomi snapped the yo-yo toward her feet. It quickly shot down the line but not back up. Instead it spun near her ankles without touching the ground. The trick was called "sleeping" the yo-yo.

Next she chanted another rhyme.

Go to sleep but not to bed.
Ride the ice back up instead.

Ian and I shared a quick look. We'd seen the yo-yo in action and knew what it could do. So I snatched the egg, and we scampered close to my sister. Something magical or dangerous was about to happen.

Splagt!

Make that something magical *and* dangerous.

A torrent of milky liquid sprayed out of the yo-yo like water rushing over a falls. It splattered the ground at our feet and froze instantly.

"What's this?" I muttered, glancing at the floor.

Gurnk!

Then it suddenly lurched upward, and Naomi, Ian, and I were whisked toward the ceiling. It was nearly impossible to keep standing.

"I hope you know how to stop!" I shouted at Naomi.

The floor wasn't rising, and the ceiling wasn't dropping. Naomi was making a pillar of ice beneath us. The taller it grew, the higher we soared.

The whole scene made me think of a giraffe stretching its neck to reach the highest branch.

"Here we fly!" Naomi cheered. The sparkle in her eyes was a bonfire.

You're going to kill us! I wanted to scream.

The pillar continued to grow, and we continued to rise. Soon we shot through the hole in the ceiling and were back in the cavern above.

"Jump!" Naomi cried. "Make like a frog!"

I glanced at her. *A frog?* Frogs hopped. It was a strange thought at a strange time.

But she didn't give me time to puzzle it out. She just shouted and then shoved. First Ian and then me, right between the shoulder blades. We fell from the pillar, kicking like kids being tickled by older siblings.

Bamph! Whamph! Tamph!

The three of us landed one after the other. Ian and I

grunted as we hit the ice. Naomi giggled breathlessly.

"Wasn't that fun?" she asked. By her tone, I expected her to follow with, "Let's do it again!"

I groaned wordlessly and heaved the egg off my chest. Amazingly it hadn't broken in the fall. I guess I was too big and cushy a target to miss.

That meant the baby dragon was still safe and still staring. Blink, blink. I was beginning to think it was in love with me.

"Chicken lizard," I muttered again.

Naomi was the first back on her feet. "We're almost back to Erzua's," she said cheerfully. "When we get there, let me do the talking." With that, she brushed the snow off her knees and started walking.

I winked at Ian. "Like we have a choice," I whispered. Naomi always did the talking.

Ian nodded then dropped to all fours and bounded after my sister. He clearly wasn't in the mood for jokes.

Not that I blamed him. Dealing with a dragon was dangerous business. Taking it lightly could be fatal.

In minutes we reached Erzua's lair, and Naomi held up a hand.

"Stay together," she instructed. "And keep your mouths shut."

Before we could protest, she flashed a smile and spun away. Her pigtails bounced as she jogged into the dragon's library of a lair.

"Erzua!" she called. "We have your egg!"

Grumbling, Ian and I dashed after her. Running hadn't been a part of the plan, and I couldn't be expected to keep up. I was carrying a blinking chicken-lizard!

Grr-RARRRG!

Erzua came to my rescue.

Sort of.

Without warning, she appeared almost on top of me. Her claws tore into the icy ground. Her fierce eyes bored into mine.

"Going somewhere?" she challenged, and her voice was like a queen's. She expected to be heard and obeyed. "Give the egg to me."

The New Deal

28

Knees suddenly weak, I stumbled backward and took a sharp breath. The egg in my arms felt heavier than ever, and Erzua's gaze heavier still.

She was watching me the way a cat watches a cornered mouse. With confidence and a smirk. I was a plaything to her, caught and helpless. Soon I would be dinner.

"The egg?" she repeated coolly.

I took another step back and stiffly shook my head. I defied her! My courage amazed even me.

"*N*-no," I stammered. "Not until we get Ian's answer."

The dragon cocked her head, and a slow smile showed her teeth. She was surprised and amused. The glassy sound of laughter vibrated in her throat again.

"That was not our deal," she purred. "Need I remind you?" Her voice was sweet, sickeningly sweet. Like drinking a glass of honey. "It was the egg for an answer, and I do not yet have the egg."

Then she thrust her face near mine, and her icy breath numbed my skin. I wasn't a cornered mouse anymore. Now I was a pig on a platter.

"Give the egg to me," she demanded.

My mouth worked, but I couldn't find any words. Naomi had them as usual.

"Don't do it, Noah!" she cried. "Erzua won't keep the deal. Look at all these frozen people."

Her words made me colder than Erzua's breath. We knew almost nothing about the dragon. What made us believe that she would keep a deal with us? We would likely end up in our own blocks of ice.

"We want the answer first," Naomi told the dragon. "Then you'll get the egg. We—"

Erzua didn't allow her to say more.

"SILENCE!" she bellowed, and just like that, I was forgotten. She spun in a lightning half-circle and snatched Naomi in a huge scaly claw.

"Your mouth is TROUBLE!" the dragon declared, her roar getting louder. "For that there will be no deal. The dog would have gone free with its answer. Now all of you will stay."

She couldn't have been any clearer. Erzua had never planned to let all of us go. Her deal had been with Ian, not Naomi and me. We were just insignificant pawns.

Erzua threw back her head and sucked in a gigantic

breath. Only Ian stopped what she was about to do.

Arrrr-roooo!

He leaped overhead from somewhere behind me. His shadow flickered past like a bow shot. Then, falling, he stretched to his limit and caught Erzua's wing in his teeth.

The dragon shrieked and spun again. She was wild and in pain, not attacking this time. Her tail swatted books and prisoners in ice. Ian had discovered a weakness.

"PUNISHMENT IS DUE!" she roared, and plumes of frost chugged from her nostrils. "ETERNITY IN ICE!"

A sudden chill clutched my spine, and I glanced around the cavern. There were dozens of prisoners, all frozen alive. Three more would make little difference.

And why should they? Nothing we had done had made a difference yet. Not sailing across the sea, not battling the necrowhal, not rescuing Erzua's egg. Nothing had—

Erzua's egg! That was it. How simple and perfect. I had everything I needed to make the most important difference.

Stormfall almost jumped into my hands and felt as light as a balloon. How I'd ever struggled with it seemed so far away. The hammer was mine now, and that would save us.

I raised it above my head and took aim. Then I yelled for the dragon.

"Erzua, stop!"

But there was no response, and the battle raged on.

"Stop!" I repeated louder, hoping not to stumble on my lie. "Stop or I will smash your egg."

29

The dragon froze, and so did my friends. Wide eyes on me, jaws slack and opened.

I had just threatened to destroy Erzua's egg. What a way to attract attention.

I stood motionless as they stared, legs spread and arms raised. Stormfall glinted in my hands. The egg sat helpless at my feet. All I needed to do was bring the hammer down.

Not that I would do such a thing. No, never. Just the idea made me sick. There was a baby in that egg, and dragon or not, I couldn't harm it.

But Erzua didn't know that, and I prayed I could fool her. It was the only chance we had. Three kids couldn't win a real fight with a dragon.

"First," I began, struggling to keep my voice steady. "Let my friends go."

I thought that would do it, start our escape. The request

was simple and clear. Don't hurt my friends, and I won't hurt the egg. It seemed fair to me.

But Erzua wasn't convinced. Her eyes narrowed, studying me, and a new chill sank into my bones. Under that gaze, I felt as brittle and transparent as an icicle.

"Harm the egg and die," she rasped.

Just like that, she called my bluff. She didn't believe that I would hurt the egg. She had seen into my heart, and her gaze was so very cold.

I shuddered and my knees threatened to buckle. This was the end. The cold was too much. Erzua had already won.

So very cold …

"Do it, Noah."

For the first time in the cavern, my sister didn't shout. She spoke firmly yet softly, and I had never heard her more clearly.

"Do it," she repeated. "Show her we mean business."

The cold inside me evaporated like a mirage. I was me again, warm and sure. And I was ready for Erzua.

Thanks to Naomi, I told myself. I owed her yet again.

Without a word, I struck with my boot. The egg wobbled, creaked, and then fell onto its side. A shallow chip marred its surface.

"This isn't a game," I told Erzua. "Let my friends go, or I'll use the hammer next."

A long silence passed between us. The dragon stared at me, and I stared right back. We could have been the only two in the cavern.

Finally Erzua sighed. Now she believed me.

"So be it," she growled. "Your friends for the egg."

I shook my head. "You owe us an answer, too," I reminded her. "And I'm keeping the egg until we get it." Then to prove my point, I hung Stormfall on my belt and scooped up the egg.

Erzua nodded, and a second later Naomi and Ian crossed the ice to join me. Together we started shuffling backward toward the exit.

"Your question?" the dragon asked, and her icy tone left no doubt. She would kill us if given the chance—slowly. Only the egg was keeping us alive.

Knowing that, Ian spoke up. "How do I break my curse?"

To our surprise, Erzua laughed. Not the musical tinkling in her throat but a hearty guffaw. Her sides even shook with mirth.

"You cannot," she chortled. "Now give the egg to me."

Naomi, of course, would have none of that. She raised an arm and pointed the mitten that was so often pointed at me.

"That's not an answer!" she protested. "If Ian can't break the curse, tell us who can."

The dragon laughed harder at this, her lips curling in a reptilian smile. Even threatened and cornered, she remained in control.

"Perhaps the cur asked the wrong question," she suggested slyly. "His curse may not be what he thinks."

Naomi frowned and jabbed her hand forward. "Call it what you want," she said. "A curse, a disease—whatever. Just tell us how to help him."

Erzua clucked her tongue, still amused. We had the egg, but she had the answers. We were like a pair of wrestlers locked in one another's grip.

"Travel to North Village," she said at last. "You will find more answers there." Then her voice lowered significantly. "Here you will find an enemy."

The threat in her words was clear. Leave. Now. Before she risked the safety of her egg to destroy us.

"Let's go," I called to my sister. "We got what we came for."

To my relief, she nodded. So did Ian. The two of them nearly sprinted for the exit.

"Hurry!" Naomi urged as she ran past.

I nodded but took my time. There was one thing left to do.

When I was sure my friends had reached the exit, I plunked the egg onto the ice. Two glassy eyes stared at me. Blink, blink.

"So long, chicken-lizard," I muttered. Then I clutched Stormfall and brought up my arms.

Slickery Trickery

30

"Stop!" Erzua roared. "Do not harm the egg!"

She was charging across the cavern toward me as if trying to outrun a wildfire. Her wings strained, propelling her forward. Her claws tore chunks from the ground. She was a frost-snorting stampede of one.

This is it, I thought in that instant. There would be no freezing and no block of ice. Erzua had one plan, and that was death.

Yet somehow I held my ground, and somehow I started to swing.

"Keep back!" I yelled, but I couldn't say more. There wasn't time to explain. Stormfall was arcing and coming down fast.

Whoolm!

When it struck, the whole world went white. Erzua vanished, the egg disappeared, and the cavern faded like shadows into darkness. Blinding, burning light filled my eyes.

I was flying, too, tossed like driftwood on the cusp of a wave. Backward I hurtled until—

"Gungh!"

I crashed into my friends.

"Hurry, hurry!" I heard Naomi pleading. "Get up!"

Strong hands caught me under the arms and lifted me to my feet.

"*I*-I'm …" I stumbled, dizzy in body and mind, "I'm all right."

Nevertheless, I winced as my vision returned. My eyelids were chapped and raw.

"You're all right?" Naomi snapped. "*All right!* You almost blew us down to Icefathom Deep!"

I ignored her and blinked gingerly, trying to clear my eyes. As details became clear, I discovered that part of what she had said was true. I really had blown us backward.

We were in the tunnel that used to lead to Erzua's lair. *Used to* because a cave-in blocked the entrance. Now the only way to go was out.

Which is perfect, I thought happily, and gave Stormfall a pat. The hammer had done exactly what I'd wanted.

By striking the ground, I had caused the ceiling in Erzua's lair to collapse. She and her egg were trapped inside. Digging out of that much snow and ice would take time.

Gunga-dun-doon!

Time that not even we had. Because by the sound of it, the whole tunnel was about to collapse.

"Run!" I shouted. "You can yell at me later!"

I gave Ian a shove and grabbed Naomi's hand. We had minutes, maybe seconds, to escape the tunnel. Clumps of snow were already falling like dirt in an unstable mineshaft.

"Don't stop for any—!"

I bit my tongue before finishing.

In front of us stood the frozen ogress. We couldn't avoid her or stopping.

"Halllp me," she pleaded.

"Start climbing!" Ian barked, but I had other plans.

Reaching for Stormfall, I charged. The hammer would be my battering ram. Because this time I wasn't going over. My plan was to take the ogress with us.

Thromp!

Too bad that plan didn't work quite the way I wanted. When Stormfall connected, the block didn't break. It fell over like a log. All I did was knock the poor ogress onto her face!

"Leedle peeples," she moaned, still trapped.

"That wasn't … I'm *s*-sorry," I babbled.

First I'd swung so hard that I almost brought the mountain down. Then I'd pecked the ogress as gently as a kiss from grandma. Was there anything in between?

"Be quiet and get on," Naomi said, taking charge. There wasn't time for apologies or to fix what had happened. The ceiling was about to fall on our heads.

Get on meant *stay on*, I soon found out. Because next Naomi started to spin her yo-yo and recite another rhyme.

A slippery trick is what we need.
Make trickery slick, to build up speed.

Afterward she shouted, "Hang on!"

We did, and her hands moved rapidly in a trick called "rocking the cradle." First she formed a triangle with the yo-yo's string. Then she dangled the yo-yo inside it. All the while, the yo-yo continued to spin.

Impressive but unhelpful, and I let her know.

"We don't need tricks," I said. "Where's the magic?"

Skloo-oo-oo!

For an answer, we started to move.

A stream of water squirted from the yo-yo, hit the ground ahead of us, and froze. Seconds later, the block of ice was sliding down the new ice like a toboggan, taking us with it.

"Carpe draco!" Naomi cheered. Then to me, she added, "You should trust me more."

I almost laughed. *Trust her?* Didn't she realize that her secret weapon was a yo-yo? A paddleball and jump rope couldn't be far behind.

Still, there we went speeding down the tunnel. Naomi kept her trick going, and the yo-yo kept squirting water.

131

Not bad, I had to admit. I was kind of proud of my sister.

But our good fortune didn't last. The block of ice didn't have brakes or a steering wheel.

So when the tunnel turned sharply ahead, we had a fast choice to make. Crash into the wall or jump while moving at breakneck speed.

31

Wall or jump? Wall or jump? It really wasn't much of a choice. We could abandon our ice block sled and try to run. Or we could hit the wall and hope to break through.

Both options were dangerous, but staying in the tunnel was worse. Its ceiling was quaking, and its walls cracking. Soon it would be as roomy as a flattened igloo.

"Brace yourselves!" I cried, making a decision. We had to stay with the sled. Escaping on foot would be impossible.

"Brace—*what?*" Naomi demanded. Her eyes widened, and her mouth fell open. For once she didn't have anything else to say.

Twenty feet from the wall, I steadied Stormfall in front of me like a lance. At ten feet, I bent my knees and squared my shoulders. At five, I screamed.

Thwoolm!

When I'd used Stormfall last, the world had turned white.

133

This time it exploded with color.

Brown rock, white ice, tan fur, grey clouds, silver metal, and blonde hair whirled dizzily around me. It was like looking into a kaleidoscope. I couldn't tell where one color ended and another began.

We were flying, that much I knew. Flying like a downhill skier after hitting a mogul. We weren't in the tunnel anymore, and we weren't in the mountain. We were—

Free!

"We made it!" I cheered, fairly astonished.

Ramming the wall had been the right thing to do. We had broken through it to safety.

Bloomp!

Our block of ice hit the ground as flatly as a slap on the knee. Straight onto the snowy mountainside. From there it started to slide rapidly downhill, more like a toboggan than ever.

As we descended, a wintry breeze chilled our cheeks, and flurries peppered our hair. We could see for miles and imagine more. The snowy horizons were endless.

"What fun!" Naomi exclaimed, and Ian howled in agreement.

Only the ogress wasn't enjoying herself. She remained facedown in the ice and was probably wondering what awful thing would happen next.

"Leeeeeedle peeeeeeples!" she yowled helplessly.

"Not much longer!" I shouted to her. "We're almost to

the bottom."

"Don't worry," Naomi added. "We'll get you out of there."

Not five minutes away from the dragon's lair, and my sister's mouth was getting us into trouble again. I had no idea how to free the ogress. Using Stormfall hadn't worked.

But at that moment, I had other things to worry about. Other things like whales, believe it or not.

Yes, whales. Whoolyback whales to be precise.

North of Bargain Mountain, a wide channel ran east and west across the snowy plains. It cut through the ground like a river canyon and was completely filled with powdery snow. In it swam the whales.

The channel was called Snowshoe Divide, and no one knew how deep it was. Its banks were at least a jousting field apart.

The whoolyback whales swam along it side-by-side in pairs—that's four across, and that's wide. Each whale was as big as a necrowhal.

Until today I hadn't seen one up close. The whales swam quickly and never stopped moving. So stumbling onto a whole school was just dumb luck.

Not that we literally stumbled onto them or felt that lucky about it. We sort of flew onto them. At least I remember being airborne and hearing the screams. Some of them weren't even mine.

32

"Look out!"

"Jump!"

"Left! Lean left!"

Ian, Naomi, and I shouted instructions all at once. None of them agreed, and none of them helped. It was too late to stop what was happening.

We had come to the bottom of the mountain, and our sled had no brakes. Next stop: Snowshoe Divide.

We hit the channel's near bank and launched into the air. Our shouting stopped. Our mouths and eyes went wide. We soared in utter silence, too shocked even to breathe.

Beneath us chugged the huge furry bodies of the whales. Snow churned in their wake like frothy, boiling soup. Landing in either would be the end of us.

Thwatt!

Luck·saved us. Luck and a gigantic white tail.

It struck without warning, but maybe not by accident. First a whale's massive deep blue eye caught my gaze. It stared without blinking for a timeless moment. Then the tail struck.

It sent us spiraling back the way we had come and tossed us from the sled. Ice snapped and splintered in the air. Our voices returned, and we howled in despair.

Four dull thumps marked our landing on the shore—Ian, Naomi, the ogress, and me. The block of ice was gone, smashed into pieces too small to count.

We were safely on land but not out of trouble. The ogress was free of her prison.

"Get your yo-yo!" I shouted to Naomi. "Be ready!"

As for me, I struggled to stand in the deep snow. I leaned on Stormfall for support, thankful I still wore Erzua's band on my arm.

Surprisingly, it was the ogress who spoke next. She popped up from the snow like a prairie dog from its burrow.

"Moogla no wants fight," she said in a slow, slobbery voice. "Leedle peeples saved Moogla."

So I took a risk and belted Stormfall. Moogla seemed friendly. We could be the same.

Naomi took that as her queue.

"We're going to North Village," she said. "Want to come along?"

My mouth fell open, and so did Ian's. Being polite was one thing. Inviting the ogress to tag along was another.

137

"Norff Village!" she exclaimed. "That's that-a-way!" She pointed a meaty hand over the canyon and grinned.

Naomi nodded. "I think we can hop from one whale to the next. We'll pretend it's a big game of hopscotch."

Moogla frowned, and I could almost hear her big brain chugging. Finally she shook her head.

"Bad idea," she said. "Bad, bad. One slip and leedle peeples get all smooshed. Here, Moogla help."

Before my sister could react, Moogla snatched her by the shoulders. Then the ogress spun like an athlete preparing to throw a discus.

"No, no!" Naomi cried. "Help! No—!

"Waaaaaaaaaah!"

Her call for help turned into a shriek. She was flying. Moogla had thrown her.

Enraged, I rounded on the ogress. "What have you done?" I demanded. My sister was soaring to her death.

For an answer, Moogla grabbed my shoulders and lifted me, complete with Stormfall, off the ground. I might as well have been stuffed with straw. So much for big-boned.

"Up we go!" she slobbered. Then she spun around once and tossed me too. It was my turn to fly.

I flapped my arms and kicked my legs, but neither did any good. Moogla's muscles were powering me. I would land when and where she wanted.

"Run, Ian!" I yelled, thinking those would be my last words. Someone had to live to tell my parents what had happened.

To my dismay, he responded, "Right behind you, Noah!"

He wasn't exaggerating either. The werewolf was scampering over the furry back of a whale below me. When he reached its side, he jumped to the next whale in line.

Floo-ooph!

Then I landed in powder so soft that I thought of a cloud. Who knew that drowning in snow would be so pleasant?

Gazing up, I saw Naomi looking down at me. Her rosy cheeks almost matched the light in her eyes.

"No time for sleeping," she grinned. "North Village is just ahead." Then she stuck out a hand and helped me up.

We were on the far side of Snowshoe Divide. Moogla had thrown us safely across!

Ian bounded up, tongue lolling to the right.

"I never knew something so big could fly," he teased.

That earned him a snowball square on the nose, and we both laughed.

Meanwhile, Naomi was shouting to Moogla. The ogress remained on the far bank, waving her meaty hands.

"Are you coming with us?" my sister asked.

"No, no," the ogress answered in her wet drawl. "Moogla goes home now. Time to find me brudder."

I smiled and shook my head. Never would I have imagined the ogress having a long-lost brother.

Will we meet him someday? I wondered.

"Farewell, Moogla!" Naomi exclaimed. "Thank you so

much. We owe you a huge favor!"

The ogress waved a final time, turned, and started to trudge away. We watched her plod through the snow until she was a tiny speck in the distance.

Then we turned to the hill ahead and began to climb. North Village was near. So, I was sure, was Ian's answer.

33

Ian and his keen wolfish eyesight spotted it first. North Village lay in ruins.

"I can't go farther," he announced. "Something terrible has happened. The people won't want to see me."

By that he meant the townsfolk wouldn't want a werewolf in their village. Even though he was completely trustworthy, Ian was a stranger and strange. He wouldn't be welcomed at a time like this.

"Don't worry, Ian," Naomi offered. "We'll find out why Erzua sent us here."

"Yeah," I agreed lamely. "And we'll see you in the morning."

Ian nodded but said nothing else. He just turned and dashed off into the night.

As I watched him go, I'd never felt more like a coward.

Naomi patted my arm. "Come on. There's a building up

ahead. I think I see people inside."

Shoulder to shoulder, we shuffled along the rutted street. Buildings were completely flattened on either side. Silos lay like fallen timber. Something huge must have caused the damage.

Naturally I thought of Erzua right away. She was big enough to destroy a village.

"Halt!"

A voice rang out in the darkness, as unexpected as thunder on a clear day. Until then, the village had been tomb-silent.

"Halt yourself!" Naomi challenged, glancing around and squinting. "Wherever you are."

A flutter of wings suddenly rustled to our left, and we spun in time to see the strangest bird streak past. It looked like a tiny dragon made of polished metal and multicolored feathers.

"Chicken lizard," I muttered to myself.

"I said 'halt,'" the unseen speaker continued, closer now but still hidden. "Tell me your names."

Naomi and I spun again, expecting a heavily armed guard. Instead we saw a brown-haired boy about Naomi's age. He certainly wasn't any taller than she. In fact, he was kind of puny.

On his right hand he wore a big leather glove that reached his elbow. Perched on it was the colorful dragon-bird.

"Tell me your names," the boy repeated.

Naomi opened her mouth and raised her mitten to point. Then I stepped on her toes.

"I'm Noah, and this is my sister Naomi," I said quickly. "We're here from South Village on … on a mission of peace."

Although true, that last part sounded silly even to me.

The boy nodded then cocked his head at the dragon-bird. Slowly he nodded again.

"Who are your parents, Noah?" he asked.

I told him quickly before Naomi could interject. There was no doubt that she was a pot about to boil over.

After I answered, the boy sighed with relief.

"Welcome to North Village," he said. "I'm Jasiah and this is Plume." He meant the dragon-bird on his arm. "Sorry we had to treat you like criminals. It's just so hard to tell."

Naomi put her hands on her hips. "Hard to tell what?"

Jasiah shrugged. "If you've lost your memories," he explained.

He said the words casually, as if losing memories was common. But Naomi and I gawked at one another in amazement.

Whatever had happened to Ian had happened to others. He wasn't alone. He wasn't the only one who had forgotten his past.

That meant that others could have been turned into

werewolves and were searching for answers, too. My mind reeled with hope.

"Follow me," Jasiah said. "My uncle will answer all of your questions."

34

Jasiah's Uncle Arick was the biggest man I'd ever seen. He was tall, wide, and muscular, and had a deep voice to match.

"Have you heard of the Octolith?" he asked from his seat by the door.

We were in a barn, the only large building left standing in town. People crowded one end, most sitting on blankets or hay bales. Livestock bleated and whinnied in the other end. It was very warm.

Naomi and I shook our heads. We'd never heard of the Octolith.

"It's a foul tower built on gigantic octopus-like legs," Arick explained. "It slithers across land and sea, destroying everything in its path."

"Like this village?" Naomi interjected, and Arick nodded.

"Aye, like this village. It attacked this afternoon and

kidnapped most of the residents. Those here are all that remain."

A quick look around caused me to shudder. The barn was crowded, yes, but not with enough people to populate an entire village. Most of its citizens were gone.

"What happens to the people who are taken?" I asked. I thought I knew the answer but wanted to make sure.

"Their memories are erased," Jasiah replied. "At least that's what happens to the lucky ones. Most are never seen again."

"What about werewolves?" Naomi asked. "Does the Octolith turn people into werewolves?"

Arick shrugged his broad shoulders. "Perhaps. We've seen werewolves near the tower but haven't spoken to them."

That was enough for Naomi. Lost memories and werewolves told her all she needed to know. She was ready to leave now.

"We have to find the Octolith," she told me. "That's where Ian needs to go."

I nodded, unable to disagree. Erzua had said we would find answers in the village. It seemed she had been right.

"We'll leave as soon as it's light," I promised.

Jasiah and his uncle saw that we were fed and given blankets. After that, the night passed slowly. We didn't sleep much and had no room to stretch out in the warm barn. By morning our legs and backs ached more than if we hadn't rested.

"I have something to show you," Jasiah greeted us at dawn. "Come outside."

Munching cheese and day-old bread, we followed him outside. What we saw there caused us to gasp.

The damage to the village was worse than we'd imagined. The ruts in the road hadn't been caused by wagons or heavy traffic. They were a trail left by the Octolith.

A trail that slithered north to the horizon.

"Follow that and you'll find the Octolith," Jasiah said. "I wish I could go with you."

Naomi and I agreed. Jasiah was nice, and his dragon-bird looked fierce in the daylight. The two of them would be good to have along when trouble broke out.

Not *if* trouble broke out. When. Tracking the Octolith was going to be the most dangerous thing we had ever done.

We said goodbye quickly and then started off along the trail. Ian caught up to us just outside of town.

"Sleep well?" he grinned. "Or did the pigs hog all of the blankets?"

Naomi rolled her eyes. "I suppose you found a nice doghouse to sleep in."

What a pair!

"We have to follow this trail," I said. "It leads to a tower called the Octolith."

Ian nodded and started to dash back and forth, sniffing

the trail excitedly. After several moments he sat back on his haunches and gazed at us.

"You'll never catch up," he stated. "You're too slow."

At first I thought he was making a chubby joke, but his serious tone changed my mind.

"We're going to need help," he continued. "Plug your ears." Then he lifted his head and howled.

Arrrr-roooo!

Several moments passed. Ian sat still, barely breathing. Then a pair of shapes appeared to our left. They loped toward us from a stand of evergreens, moving swiftly over the snow.

They were wolves. One was solid white except for black ears. The other was as grey as a storm cloud.

"Don't be afraid," Ian advised. "They can smell fear." His grin was particularly wolfish.

35

As the wolves approached, I stepped in front of Naomi. I wanted me between them and her. Big bones could be good for something.

"Stay calm," I whispered. Ian hadn't been joking when he'd said wolves could smell fear.

Naomi thanked me by swatting the back of my head.

"They can smell gullible too," she snorted. "We know those wolves, Noah. We saw them in the needlespine pines."

She pointed at the wolf with black ears, and I could have slapped myself. Gullible was right. Even after spending so much time with Ian, I still reacted badly to wolves. That wasn't the kind of person I wanted to be.

"This is Two Shadows," Ian introduced, nodding at the wolf with black ears. "Her big friend is Stalking Ghost."

Big friend? I gaped silently. What an understatement.

Both of the wolves stood almost as tall as my shoulders. They were the size of ponies—with fangs!

"Nice to meet you," Naomi smiled, and I managed a nod. It *was* nice to be met and not eaten. Good for the heart, too.

"Two Shadows and Stalking Ghost have agreed to let you ride them," said Ian. "It's the only—"

Just then Naomi squealed, drowning out whatever else Ian had been about to say.

"Let us ride them?" she exclaimed. "Let us ride them! Us? Ride wolves!"

She grabbed my arm like a kid pointing out the best toy in a store window. "Noah, did you hear that?"

I smiled at her, surprised to find that I was excited too. "What are we waiting for?" I grinned.

In minutes we were on our way. Naomi rode Two Shadows, and I awkwardly straddled Stalking Ghost's back. Both of us held our breath but for different reasons.

The wolves ran tirelessly, and the miles passed swiftly. We crossed windy plains, deep with drifting snow. We hurtled frozen riverbeds and zigzagged through pinewood forests.

Not once did the wolves stumble or slow. Never did they complain. They ran on and on, as strong and as dedicated as soldiers.

"Is this better than riding a frozen ogre?" Ian smirked as he sprinted alongside us.

Seeing him run, I was amazed at how comfortable and

happy he looked. On two legs or four, he always seemed at ease.

Will he miss being a werewolf? I wondered. *Will he like being a regular boy again?*

I knew I would miss the band on my arm, and wearing it was just a small change. So small that I couldn't even feel it under my parka anymore.

Having the band was nothing like being turned into a werewolf. Nevertheless the day I lost it would be dark.

How, then, would Ian feel when he couldn't run with the wolves anymore?

A short time later, Ian called a halt. We had reached the top of a broad hill shaped like a horseshoe. In a wooded valley below us stood the Octolith.

The tower loomed over the surrounding trees like a parent on a playground. We couldn't see its octopus-like legs, but it was still a forbidding sight.

Ice and rime girded it in armor. Thick blocks encircled its summit like bared teeth. Getting inside would be a challenge. Getting out would probably be a lost cause.

"Everyone ready?" I croaked. We had come a long way. There was no reason to delay now.

Naomi swallowed. "Ready."

"Ready," Ian growled.

Slowly Naomi, Ian, and I started down the hill. The wolves stayed behind, and the Octolith waited. We were on our own again.

36

Noises echoed in the valley as we shuffled down the hillside. Snow crunched beneath our feet. Branches creaked in the trees. Everything nearby seemed to be trying to speak.

Even the wind.

It started softly—a whisper here, a murmur there. Words followed, and soon complete thoughts.

"What about da gold?" demanded a gruff voice, and I turned, expecting to spot a stranger.

"Happy birthday!" cheered a crowd of voices coming from overhead.

But these voices had no bodies. They belonged to ghosts or spirits or—

Memories.

Yes, memories. We were close to the Octolith now. Close to the place where memories were stolen. It wasn't

153

impossible to imagine that a few of them had escaped.

"Will you marry me?"

"How many times must I tell you?"

"Please let the dog out."

"Let's do the slithersaur shuffle!"

The voices babbled on and on—young and old, male and female. Finally I slapped my hands over my ears.

"I can't take it!" I shouted. "Is anyone else hearing all this?"

Naomi smacked her lips. "Mmm. Blueberry-toogood," she mumbled, a faraway look on her face.

"So you hear them too?" I asked. "The voices?"

She gave me a blank look. "Voices? I don't hear any voices. But I smell blueberry-toogood!" To prove it, she started sniffing the air crazily as if following scented clues on a treasure hunt.

Ian did the same while scampering back and forth. "I smell it too!" he yelped.

And sure enough, so did I. But not just blueberry-toogood. I smelled minty pinecones, vanilla candles, smoked fish, and—*phew!*—wet dog. Scent after scent filled my nostrils as if squirted from perfume bottles.

But none of them were real, I knew. The scents were memories, just like the voices. They had escaped the Octolith and were floating around randomly.

Just wait, I told myself. *They'll probably get worse as we get closer to the tower.*

Out loud, I said, "They aren't real. Try to ignore them."

Bunched closely together, we tiptoed into the valley. Everything went fine until we reached the trees. Then Naomi saw the first thing that wasn't there.

"Look out!" she shrieked, clutching my arm and almost dragging me to the ground. "It's Erzua!"

I broke free of her grasp and squinted into the trees, my hand on Stormfall. I expected ice and wind, blue scales and yellow eyes. Instead I saw Bart and his gang lurking among the evergreens.

"Fire!" Bart bellowed, stabbing an oversized paw at us. Immediately his gang launched a dozen icy snowballs into the air.

"Haha!"

"Get 'em!"

"Attack!"

The boys howled like a pack of drooling hyenas, and avoiding their assault was impossible. Bart had planned the perfect ambush. All I could do was close my eyes and brace for impact.

"Noah, behind you!" Ian barked.

Before the snowballs struck, I whirled and opened my eyes. *Now what?* I wanted to shout. This day couldn't possibly get worse.

Splack!

Wrong! The day could get worse. Worse and gross.

A pasty blue tentacle as long as a dragon's tail swatted

155

me across the chest. Gooey strands stretched between it and me. Slime soaked my coat. The blow sent me stumbling backward, my arms flailing for balance.

Ian caught me before I fell, and Naomi rushed to join us. All our eyes stared straight ahead. We had found the Octolith.

Gone were the ghostly threats and memories. Bart, his gang, and their snowballs vanished. Erzua disappeared. The dreamy voices and scents faded like the details of a dream.

All that remained was the Octolith—giant, icy, and alive. A mass of tentacles like tangled anacondas writhed at its base. They kept the tower standing and creeping ever forward.

"How are we supposed to get inside?" Naomi pondered.

The Octolith didn't have a door or windows, and I was surprised it didn't have a mouth. The tower was like a living thing. Didn't that mean it had to eat?

Splack!

Suddenly a tentacle shot out, snatching Naomi in its grip. It coiled around and around her waist, then lifted her off the ground.

She screamed, I screamed, and Ian howled in vain. The Octolith was about to demonstrate exactly how it got its food.

37

"Charge!" I roared, tearing Stormfall from my hip and starting to run.

This time I wasn't seeing things. The Octolith was real. Its tentacles clutched my sister, lifting her steadily higher. That wouldn't change if I blinked, no matter how much I wished it would.

Ian sprinted next to me, head down and fur on end. His cloak snapped behind him. His expression was a snarl.

Big-Bones and Werewolf to the rescue! I nearly cried. What an unlikely pair of heroes!

Seven tentacles met our charge, weaving side-to-side like snakes. I struck with Stormfall, and Ian leaped, fangs bared. What happened next was loud.

Splurk-splack! The tentacles slapped.

Thooom! Stormfall crashed.

Arrrr-roooo! The werewolf howled, somehow growling

at beginning and end.

The noisy battle lasted seconds. Maybe less, if possible.

Splack! A tentacle caught my arms. *Splurk!* A second snatched Ian. In a blink we were lassoed and hauled into the air.

"Hang on, Naomi!" I yelled.

"We're coming!" Ian added.

Though captured we weren't giving up. It was better to pretend that we'd let ourselves get caught.

The tentacles rushed upward, dragging us with them like fish on a line. Icy white walls raced past. Shrieking wind rivaled our screams. Wherever we were going wouldn't take long to reach.

"Almost to the top!" Ian barked, meaning the top of the tower. A moment later we passed it and then the unex- pected happened.

The tentacles let go.

Screaming again, Ian and I fell into the Octolith. There was no roof to catch us, just a gaping hole like a hungry mouth. That it didn't snap shut as we plunged in amazed me.

Still, the fall seemed to last forever and somehow take us through ages past. Voices whispered of forgotten secrets. Visions hinted at events long ago.

The things we heard and saw were memories, like before, but they were so much stronger now. Whispers turned to shouts. Colors blazed as if polished. Soon I squeezed my eyes shut and screamed to block the noise.

When my voice began to crack, I held my breath and waited. Finally there was no sound but the thumping of my heart.

I peeked open my eyes to find that I was lying in a round room. A squishy substance like marshmallow padded the floor. Narrow tentacles speckled with suction cups lined the walls in vertical stripes.

"*W*-where are we?" Naomi groaned, and I exhaled with relief. She was safe and only five feet away. So was Ian. The three of us were alive and unharmed.

But why? I wanted to ask, feeling suspicious. The Octolith could have destroyed us easily. Why had it let us live?

Ian knelt and clutched his head in his hands.

"I … I know this place," he said slowly. "I think I've been here before."

I nodded at him encouragingly, unsurprised. This was the place that had stolen his memories. No wonder some of them were coming back.

"It's almost over," I told him. "Soon you'll remember everything and be yourself again."

By *be yourself again*, I meant be a boy instead of a werewolf. But I couldn't bring myself to say that. It seemed rude and unnecessary.

Besides, Ian made a pretty good werewolf. He might miss being one.

He sighed and then flashed a grin. Never had he looked more human, even with so many teeth showing.

"Thanks. I hope you're right," he admitted.

Of course we didn't know it then, but such a hope was hopeless. Soon our plans for saving him would fall completely apart.

Octoclops Chops

38

"Look at this," Naomi called over her shoulder to Ian and me. "What do you think it is?"

As we turned, she jabbed a mitten at a dark glassy circle on the wall. It was the size of a dinner plate and set at eye level.

"Don't touch it!" Ian barked a second too late.

Naomi's fingers poked the circle, and it snapped shut like a trap. For a second there was silence, and then a sound like popping popcorn exploded throughout the room.

P-plerp! Plerp-plerp!

With every pop, new circles opened in the walls like giant eyes. Some of them winked. Some squinted. All of them stared.

"Ian, what's *h*-happening?" I muttered, rotating slowly. Nowhere in the room was safe. The circles were popping up everywhere.

Plerp! One opened in the wall to my right.

Plerp! P-plerp! Two more appeared, one ahead and one above.

"They're eyes," Ian hissed. "Octoclops eyes. Stay together and get ready to fight."

Naomi and I didn't need to be told twice. Braids flapping, my sister ran to join us. She clutched her yo-yo in a white-knuckled grip. Her face was set and rigid.

As for me, I drew Stormfall and tried to stay calm. But my muscles tensed, and my mouth went dry. Waiting for danger, I realized, could be almost as bad as the danger itself.

Not that we had to wait long.

Glomp! Gluh-guh-glomp!

Suddenly the room erupted with movement. Bluish bodies burst from the walls like zombies clawing up from the grave.

"Octoclops!" Ian howled.

A dozen monsters slithered toward us on wiggly tentacles. Their bodies resembled mounds of wet snow with a big eye in the middle and an even bigger mouth below. They stood as tall as my father and three times as wide.

Gluh-glomp! Glomp! They gibbered, oozing closer.

"Don't let them grab you!" Ian yowled. Then he crouched, snarled, and leaped.

But instead of aiming with teeth or claws, he struck with his forehead.

163

Splorp!

The octoclops splattered like a snowball thrown against a tree. Globs of slush flew right and left.

"Gross!" Naomi exclaimed. "Cover up when you sneeze!"

Ian barked a laugh and then sprang toward a second monster.

I would have laughed, too, but I didn't have time. An icy tentacle slapped across my neck and rapidly wrapped around it. Then the tentacle tightened and started to pull.

I dropped Stormfall on reflex and clawed at my neck. My air was going fast.

"Nay ... oh ...me ..." I gasped, trying to call my sister.

She didn't hear, but she saw. Her hand flicked forward sharply, firing her yo-yo. A short rhyme burst from her lips.

Even small packages
Can hold a surprise.
Mine's made of icicles.
Best cover your eyes.

The yo-yo streaked over my shoulder, narrowly missing my cheek. It buzzed past my ear like a hornet. What a close call!

But the octoclops was Naomi's target. One moment the monster had me in its clutches. Its excited gurgling puffed cold air against my back. The next, the yo-yo struck and the octoclops exploded in a sloppy mess.

Splor-p-p-p-p!

Two down, and ten to go. The odds were still against us.

"Noah!" Naomi shrieked.

Two octoclops clutched her arms, one each to the left and right. They looked ready to pull her apart like a turkey wishbone.

On the run, I scooped up Stormfall and attacked. I might have even howled. The octoclops to Naomi's right didn't stand a chance.

Splorp! Stormfall crushed it like an overripe melon. Slushy spray splattered the walls.

That was three down. Maybe we had a chance.

One hand free, Naomi whipped her yo-yo at the second attacking octoclops. Her aim was perfect, and the yo-yo sped toward the monster.

But at just the right moment, the octoclops twisted and opened its huge mouth. Naomi's yo-yo sailed straight inside.

Glomp!

Then the fang-filled mouth clamped shut like a castle gate. What went in might never come out.

"Pull!" I shouted. "Before it gets a good hold!" Saying the words made me think of a fisherman wrestling with a necrowhal on the line.

Naomi dug in her heels, and I raised Stormfall, preparing to charge. A single thought stopped me cold.

If I splatter the octoclops, will the yo-yo splatter too?

I froze, wondering, and that hesitation cost us.

Glomp! Gluh-glomp!

The remaining octoclops closed in. Their tentacles swatted us from every direction. Their bulky bodies bumped and shoved us into a tight circle.

Still we fought on. Naomi tugged, I whirled with Stormfall, and Ian used his whole body as a weapon.

Soon four octoclops were down, then five. We had splattered almost half of them.

But that wasn't enough, and it wouldn't be more. Fighting outnumbered and in such cramped space was too difficult.

When I slipped in a puddle of slush and dropped to my knees, the octoclops surged forward. Icy tentacles battered me as if I were on the losing side of a snowball fight. The blows pinned me to the ground.

Soon their bluish shapes faded and I saw only black.

39

Blump ...

Blump ...

Blump ...

I woke to being dragged down a curved hallway. Every few seconds my head hit a rough patch and—*blump!*—bounced into the air.

I'm up, I'm up, I thought, coming fully awake. I preferred a crowing rooster to having my head dribbled like a ball.

The octoclops had captured me. That was obvious. A tentacle bound my ankles. Another held my wrists above my head. Where we were going was a mystery, but at least I was alive.

Making it twice, I observed. Twice that I had been allowed to live. First by the tower, and now by the octoclops.

Someone wanted me alive, but who?

—I do.—

The voice that spoke the words was old, but not weak with age. Old as in dinosaur bones and stories told by a grandfather. It was deep and clear but unmistakably evil.

"*Huh*-who …?" I croaked, no louder than a mouse's footstep.

Only then did I fully realize that the voice hadn't spoken out loud. Its words had echoed in my mind like sounds from a dream.

—I do,— the voice repeated. —I, Ithasuma.—

This time I heard something else in the voice. Not just age or evil, but something needy and familiar. Ithasuma wanted me. It was hungry.

I shuddered at the thought. Was I about to be eaten?

—Fool,— Ithasuma rasped. —I am beyond the petty concerns of your frail body. I will not eat you, but I will feed.—

Somehow knowing that didn't make me feel better. Neither did the fact that Ithasuma could read my mind. Eat, feed—there wasn't much difference. I was on the menu.

—Indeed.— Ithasuma agreed, and then its voice was gone.

Another shudder shook my body, this one in relief. Ithasuma was not listening to my thoughts anymore. Its dark presence had vanished, leaving a strange emptiness in me.

Slowly I closed my eyes and sighed. Whatever Ithasuma was, it was more dangerous than anything we had ever encountered. Just its voice in my mind had threatened to crush me. Meeting it face-to-face might be unbearable.

But that was exactly what was going to happen. The octoclops were taking us to their master.

Soon we came to an archway that led to a second circular room. This one was bigger than the first, and probably as wide as the Octolith itself. It was also Ithasuma's throne room and an utter horror.

Overlapping bodies of humans, animals, and other things I couldn't identify were stuck in the walls. They protruded like victims caught in an avalanche. A hand here, a head there—all of them unmoving and all of them pale.

"Someone drank their blood!" Naomi gasped.

She was wrong, but I was glad to see her. Ian, too. For the first time since our capture, I spotted them in the clutches of nearby octoclops.

At least we're together, I told myself.

—For eternity, yes.—

Ithasuma's voice struck my mind like a physical blow. While louder and more forceful than before, it also had the eagerness of one who smells cookies baking.

—You and everyone here are mine,— Ithasuma continued. —You are like cattle to me.—

Those words frightened me more than anything ever had.

Ithasuma meant to keep us as food, like stores in a pantry. Maybe not for our bodies, but it could snack on—

Our minds.

Suddenly so much made sense. Ian's amnesia and the random memories floating around outside were connected. Ithasuma ate thoughts. It needed them to survive.

—Well done,— it congratulated dryly. —Your mind is sharp and sweet. I will save it for last. For dessert.—

I'd been frightened before. Now I was sick. What Ithasuma had described was monstrous. Not only Ian had lost memories. Everyone trapped in the walls had too. They were being used to keep the creature alive.

"We're going to stop you," I whispered, meaning it. The time had come for Ithasuma to pay for its barbaric crimes.

40

—Stop me?— Ithasuma sneered. —Ridiculous! I devoured the werewolf's mind once, and yet the animal returned. You will be no different.—

So that confirmed it. Ian *had* been here before, and Ithasuma had stolen his memories. This was where it had all begun, and this was where it would end.

Ithasuma squatted upon a low arch in the middle of the room. The arch was suspended over a round pit and made of silver-veined marble. From our angle, we couldn't see into the pit.

The creature itself had a mushroom-shaped head with no mouth or nose. Most of its body was hidden in a deep cloak. Tentacles squirmed where its legs should be, and its hands ended in hotdog-length tentacles instead of fingers.

—What makes you think that you can resist me?— it challenged.

Trapped as we were, it would have been easy to agree. We couldn't resist Ithasuma. The creature was too powerful, and no one would blame us for giving up after we'd tried so hard.

But everything Ithasuma said was wrong. Ian wasn't an animal. He wasn't even a real werewolf. Something had to be done, and we were the ones to do it.

"Ready, Ian?" I asked, a shout more than a question. We had planned for this moment on the hillside earlier. Ian knew it was coming.

"Ready, Noah," he growled fiercely.

"Ready," my sister added.

It was time, our time, and the beginning of the end of Ithasuma.

Arrrr-roooo!

Ian howled, and Naomi and I joined him. We didn't hold back and we weren't embarrassed. We wanted to make a lot of noise. That was the point.

Within seconds, there came a reply. Two voices joined ours. Two Shadows and Stalking Ghost started to howl. The wolves had known this was coming, too.

How exactly they got inside the Octolith, I didn't know. But we had found a way in, and so had they.

Two Shadows dashed into the room, her black ears flat against her head. Stalking Ghost ran close behind, and the rest of their pack followed.

In all, nine wolves joined the fight. Nine voices howled

with us. Now the odds were in our favor.

When Ithasuma saw the wolves, the creature became instantly enraged. Its chalky skin darkened. Its eyes smoldered orange. Standing on the tips of its tentacles, it screeched.

—Get them!—

The octoclops bodyguards dropped us and squirmed into action. They saw the wolf pack as a bigger threat, and maybe they were right.

Two Shadows attacked first, showing her pack how it was done. Fangs bared, she sprang onto the nearest octoclops as I'd seen Ian do so many times before.

The startled monster tried to defend itself. Up came its tentacles, cracking like whips. But Two Shadow's fierce strength was too much.

Splorp!

She collided with the octoclops, and the monster exploded into slush.

Six down! I cheered silently, adding to our total. The octoclops didn't stand a chance.

—Come to me, my warriors. Protect me and the brain!—

Ithasuma continued to shriek from its spot on the arch. Its shrill voice was like a spoiled child's now, whiny and sharp. Hearing it made my eyes throb on the inside.

Worse, the creature was calling for help, and more octoclops slithered into the room. Sometimes they came alone, sometimes in pairs. Soon we were outnumbered by more than two-to-one.

"Follow me!" I cried, beckoning Ian and my sister.

Two Shadows and her pack could handle the octoclops. It was up to the rest of us to stop Ithasuma.

"Charge!"

41

Three against one. The odds hardly seemed fair. But when Ithasuma was the one, fair had nothing to do with it.

The creature ate thoughts instead of food. Thousands of memories were trapped in its mind. For all we knew, our three-to-one was really one million-to-three.

—Correct,— Ithasuma agreed smugly. —You're outnumbered. Give up. Do not make me destroy you.—

I shook my head angrily and slapped my hands over my ears. Ithasuma was still listening to my thoughts, and using what it heard against me.

"Go away!" I shouted. "Stay out of my head!"

Fortunately Ian saw my distress and came to my rescue. Shouting orders, he put his head down and fearlessly charged the creature.

"Noah, go right!" he barked like a general. "Naomi, left. I'll take the middle."

That got my attention and kept me focused. We had a job to do, and that was to defeat Ithasuma. We couldn't let the creature's tricks distract us.

"Yes, sir!" Naomi responded, jumping into a sprint. "*Carpe draco!* Right, Noah?"

"*Um*, sure," I huffed. "*Carpe draco!*" Running and talking weren't a good combination for me. For some silly reason, I preferred breathing.

We sped forward in a triangular wedge. Ian led the way. Naomi and I followed slightly behind and to the sides.

Standing on the arch, Ithasuma calmly watched us approach. Slowly its arms came up and its snake-like fingers wriggled. Then its dry voice hissed in our minds.

Fear and terror
Deep inside
Call forth shadows
That reside
Lost and buried,
Shame-denied,
Down where courage
Fled to hide.

The words echoed confusingly as if repeated by many voices. Some were loud, some quiet. Some were male and others female. None spoke at just the same time. When they faded, my ears were ringing.

Worse, Ian was screaming as if someone had cut off his tail. Wildly he jumped, but not onto the arch or toward

Ithasuma. He leaped at something that didn't seem real.

A large ghostly figure appeared in front of him, crouching and ready to pounce. It had a hairy werewolf's body but was transparent and outlined by a faint blue glow.

"Ghost!" I cried. "It's a ghost! This place is haunted!"

Naomi screamed next. I thought she was alarmed by my words or frightened by the ghost. Then I saw her attack.

"Play nice or be *ice!*" she roared. At the same time, she snapped her arm forward and sent her yo-yo flying.

Quashh!

Straight into a second ghost.

"They're everywhere!" I exclaimed. New ghosts kept appearing as if we had disturbed an ancient burial ground.

But not all of them were werewolves. Just the one attacking Ian. Those that surrounded Naomi were giant cockroaches as big as cats. They scuttled across the floor, circling her like a school of sharks.

Not roaches! I cringed. It couldn't get worse. Naomi hated cockroaches more than anything else.

"I'm co—!" I started to tell her, but the words stuck in my throat.

Yet another ghost appeared, this one humanoid and grotesquely fat. It quivered as it lumbered toward me and looked like flesh-colored pudding come to life.

I wanted to scream, but seeing it took my breath away. This new ghost looked like me. It *was* me. Between its rolls of fat, I saw my own face staring back at me.

My thoughts whirled. *Am I seeing the future?* I worried. *Is that what I'll look like when I'm older?*

The idea terrified me. I'd been big-boned my whole life. Would it just get worse? The ghost was as blubbery as a walrus, and its stubby limbs were like tree stumps.

"No!" I wailed, stumbling to a halt and lowering Stormfall. "It can't be. No, no, no!"

We were doomed, and our grim futures were plain to see. I would grow impossibly fat. Ian would stay a werewolf. And Naomi would—

Become a cockroach?

I blinked at the thought. Ridiculous! It couldn't possibly be true.

My being fat made sense. So did Ian remaining a werewolf. But Naomi was afraid of roaches, not afraid of turning into one. The ghosts attacking her had to represent something else.

As I searched for an answer, Ithasuma's words came to mind.

Fear and terror
Deep inside
Call forth shadows
That reside …

That was it! The ghosts weren't ghosts. They were fears. *Shadowfears!* They were like ghosts but made to spook one certain person.

Ithasuma had reached into our brains to create the perfect monster for each of us. It had plucked out the things that scared us most and given life to our fears.

And now we had to fight them.

42

The blubbery shadowfear attacked suddenly. My mind was still swimming and figuring things out. I barely had time to leap out of the way.

Palmph!

Meaty fists the size of holiday hams pulverized the ground where I'd stood. One swat like that, and I would be finished.

"S-t-a-n-d s-t-i-l-l," the shadowfear moaned, its deep voice sounding choked and short of breath.

No surprise there! I told myself. *It's too fat to breathe. Probably snores like an ogre, too.*

But with amazing speed, it turned and struck again. The monster might not breathe well, but it moved faster than I imagined.

Luckily I was faster this time. Up came Stormfall to block the blow.

Palmph!

Hammer and fists clashed noisily. Powerful vibrations stung my hands, but I held on and held my ground.

Next we circled one another slowly, looking for an advantage. I crouched like a swordsman ready to spring. The shadowfear shuffled like a little boy in his father's boots. Its clumsy feet never left the ground.

"N-o-t s-o f-a-s-t," it huffed, and I realized something awful. We sounded alike. Its voice was mine! Ignore the wheezing, and listening to it was like listening to me.

Realizing that, I went berserk. Seeing my face in its bloated visage had been bad. Hearing it speak in my voice was too much.

I charged.

"No!" I howled. "I will never be you!"

Instead of raising Stormfall, I hooked the hammer to my belt. I ran with my arms wide as if to tackle the shadowfear.

Nothing logical went through my mind. I had no plan or thought to defend myself. I just wanted to attack with my bare hands. I was out of my head.

"Never you!" I kept roaring. "Never you!"

We collided, and I expected an explosion. We were polar bears fighting for territory on the icy planes. We were comets hurtling through space. We—

Were one.

There was no explosion, just a long, airy sigh. My

182

shoulder struck the shadowfear's chest. My hands wrestled with its fleshy sides. Then I started to squeeze, and the monster just disappeared.

A sharp chill surged up my spine and shot into my skull as if I had eaten ice cream too fast. The unexpected sensation drove me to my knees.

"Never," I panted, my head drooping with exhaustion.

I had defeated the shadowfear, but it wasn't gone. It was back in my head and would always be there. It was part of me. It was one of my fears. The trick was to never let it control me.

"Don't be afraid!" I shouted to my friends. "Naomi, Ian—listen to me!"

I climbed to my feet and started to run. Ithasuma was still waiting.

"Don't be afraid!"

But as I neared Ithasuma's arch, what I saw made me afraid. It was horrible and disgusting, and it pulsed as if alive.

Beneath the arch was a circular pit as wide as an icerigger. Inside it was something that resembled a huge jellyfish. It had pale, transparent skin, and lights flashed in its gooey depths like lightning above the clouds.

"It's a brain," I muttered, feeling queasy. "A giant brain. That must be where Ithasuma keeps the thoughts it steals."

—Indeed.— The creature's cold voice intruded on my thoughts again. —And your sister's mind will make a tasty

183

addition.—

I tore my eyes away from the brain and glanced up the arch. At the top stood Ithasuma. My sister knelt limply beside it.

"Naomi, get up!" I yelled.

She didn't budge. She couldn't. Ithasuma clutched her head in its tentacle-like fingers. All Naomi could do was scream, but she didn't make a sound.

43

"Let her go!" I cried. Useless, I know, but I couldn't help myself. The words just came out.

Ithasuma clutched my sister's head with both of its hands now. A sickly green glow surrounded them, and the creature chanted harsh words in a strange language.

Still on her knees, Naomi sagged under that sinister grasp. If the creature released her, I was sure she would collapse.

—It is almost finished,— Ithasuma told me. —Her memories are becoming mine. Just like the dog's.—

For the first time, I noticed Ian laying at the creature's feet. He was curled into a ball and whimpering like a puppy.

"How?" he asked no one. "How didn't I know?"

But Ithasuma wasn't finished gloating yet.

—Look,— it commanded. —See for yourself.—

Somehow I knew that it meant the brain. Evidence of what was happening to Naomi would be there.

So I looked and was horrified.

More lights flashed in the brain than before. They winked like raindrops splashing in a puddle. And in every flash, a picture appeared for an instant.

Flash!

I saw my father holding a baby-sized spoonful of mashed vegetables. He was smiling and looked quite young.

Flash!

There was my mother, tucking in the blankets at bedtime. Her mouth was opened as if singing, and I'd never seen her look prettier.

Flash!

And there I was, except it wasn't the real me. It was a muscular version of me in perfect shape and proportion. I was fit, strong, and whirling Stormfall over my head. A swarm of dracopedes surrounded me.

That actually happened! I gasped. *Everything but the muscular part.*

In fact, all of the scenes in the pictures had happened. They were memories, I realized. Naomi's memories. I was seeing the past the way she remembered it.

And Ithasuma was stealing those memories! It was sucking them out of her head.

"Let her go!" I repeated, leaping into a sprint.

In a dozen steps, I reached the top of the arch. Ithasuma

met me there, laughing.

—You will share her fate, child,— it declared. —Prepare to be—

I didn't allow it to finish. There had been enough talk and enough of Ithasuma's tricks. It was time for action.

Thwoolm!

Heaving with all my strength, I brought Stormfall down on the arch. As I'd hoped, it shattered like a glass ornament and we fell.

Straight into the pit. Straight onto the brain.

Glurk! Glapp! Glook! Glup!

Four wet slaps signaled our landing, and the brain gurgled like a hot water bottle. If it had had a mouth, I was sure it would have belched.

"Eww!" Naomi groaned, coming to her senses. "Thanks for the slimy rescue."

I smiled briefly to myself. I knew how she really felt. To her, I was muscular and strong. I was her big brother, a hero. And that was all right.

"I see you still have your mouthy memories," I teased. "Those didn't get sucked out."

Just because I knew how she felt about me didn't mean I had to tell her I knew. That would spoil the fun for both of us.

Naomi raised her hand, pointing a mitten at me. Her mouth opened to let me have it, but Ian interjected.

"Quit chatting. This fight's not over yet."

His tone caught my attention more than his words. He wasn't whimpering anymore, and he wasn't curled up on the floor. In fact, he sounded stronger and more determined than ever.

He sounded grown-up.

"Charge!" he howled, and I couldn't disobey.

Neither could Naomi. She attacked immediately. Swinging her yo-yo around-the-world, she blurted a rhyme:

Round and round and round it goes
Hurling snow and icy blows.

Ian joined her on the attack. As Naomi rhymed and whirled, he leaped. It was his trademark move.

Arrrr-roooo!

Yo-yo and werewolf struck at the same time. It was frost and fangs versus magic and memories. Something had to give.

And that something was Ithasuma. It gave them nothing to hit.

Frew! Fwoo!

First Naomi's yo-yo and then Ian missed the mark. Both passed harmlessly through the creature as if it were a ghost.

No, not a ghost! I realized right away. I had already made that mistake with the shadowfears.

Ithasuma wasn't a ghost. It was thoughts and memories come to life. It was a dream, a nightmare. Only one thing about it was real.

The brain.

That was it. The key to everything. The brain was the real Ithasuma, and the only part that mattered. Stop it and everything else would stop, too.

Yet Ithasuma wasn't finished. It howled with laughter at my friends' failed attack, and a thousand terrified voices shrieked with it.

—You are outnumbered *and* outmatched,— Ithasuma screeched. —I will have you in my collection. *Now!*—

44

Thwo-oo-olm!

Swinging harder and faster than I ever had, I brought Stormfall down. When it connected, the world around us exploded.

Thwo-oo-olm!

There was only one way to defeat Ithasuma, I discovered. The strange creature could avoid our magic and dodge our attacks. It could become as thin as a ghost.

But it could not protect its weak spot from us, or from Stormfall. So I ignored the creature and attacked the brain instead.

That was Ithasuma's weakness. The brain beneath our feet was real and solid. All of the creature's mysterious power was there, along with so many people's memories. Even Ian's secrets were hidden there, too.

Thwo-oo-olm!

One hit was all it took to change that. One blow defeated the creature and free the minds of thousands. But I swung Stormfall four times just because it felt right.

Thwo-oo-olm!

Then I dropped the hammer and threw myself over Naomi. Since she thought of me as a heroic big brother, I decided to act like one.

At first the explosion that followed was lumpy and wet. Harmless, really. Damp clumps splattered us like the snowballs thrown by Bart and his gang.

Soon, however, the second explosion began. This one wasn't wet or lumpy. It was cold, angry, and afraid.

"I want my mommy!" a child wailed hopelessly.

"*W*-where is this place?" cried an adult.

Dozens of frightened voices whispered and whined pathetically at the same time. Without doubt, they belonged to Ithasuma's victims. They were the voices of the people who had had their memories stolen.

Now those people were free and had their memories back.

"How long have we been here?"

"Am I dead or alive?"

But only one voice managed to send a chill up my spine and give me hope. The words it spoke were almost impossible to believe.

"Ian?" it gasped. "Is that really you?"

The voice belonged to a woman, and barely a moment

passed before Ian responded.

"*M*-mother?" he whispered hoarsely.

Hearing him, I cheered. His nightmare was over! Ian had his memories back, and his mother was here.

As excited as I was, I still hadn't moved. Naomi was stuck beneath me. She squirmed and slugged my shoulder.

"Get off me," she grunted. "Didn't you hear that? We won, Noah. We beat Ithasuma."

Pushing and shoving, we untangled ourselves and stood up. What we saw, however, almost knocked us back down. So much had changed!

Ithasuma was gone. So were the one-eyed octoclops. They had vanished like forgotten memories. Destroying the brain had done that.

Still, the room was more crowded than ever. People and animals of all kinds wandered around in confusion.

"Where did they come from?" Naomi asked.

"The walls," I answered, putting it together. "Remember? There were people stuck in the walls."

Now the walls were as smooth as ice, and not one person remained trapped inside them. Defeating Ithasuma had completely freed its victims, not just their minds.

Across the room I spotted Ian. He was hugging his furry mother. Among everything else in the tower, he was one thing that hadn't changed. At least not on the outside.

Ian was still a werewolf.

Suddenly my legs trembled, and I sat down before I fell.

The meaning of what I was seeing sank in hard.

Ian was a werewolf. A *real* werewolf. He had been one his whole life. There was never a curse, and Ithasuma hadn't changed him. Ian had just forgotten who he was.

Worse, we had helped him believe a lie.

"It's our fault," I muttered. "We should have known. *I* should have known."

So many times I had seen the clues. So many little things had told me that Ian was too good at being a werewolf to be anything else.

But not once did Naomi or I suggest the truth. Ian told us that he was cursed, and we believed that. We hadn't even considered that he might not look exactly like us.

Was being a werewolf bad? Was being different a curse?

I hung my head and sighed. The answer to both questions was *no*. Ian was a great person. That was what mattered, not what he looked like.

He spotted me and bounded over with his mother. A third werewolf with some grey in its fur followed. It was his father.

"Thank you," Ian said. "I know who I am again." He paused and tapped his chest with a paw. *"Carpe draco."*

And that said it all. Ian had his memories back, and he had discovered who he really was. More importantly, he was all right with it. He accepted himself inside and out.

I smiled at him and nodded. Our adventure was almost over. It was time to go home.

45

Three days later I was standing on the sidelines of the snowy field outside South Village. Naomi and I were home again, and life was returning to normal.

A little too normal, if you asked me.

"Keep your head up out there," Naomi advised. "Don't be an easy target."

As usual, she was motoring her mouth and acting like my coach. Nearby our parents watched us in amused silence, smiling to themselves.

Everything was back to normal, all right. Even Bart glared at me from across the field. Soon he would get another chance to whollop me.

Or so he thought. He didn't know about my secret weapon.

I hadn't thought of it in days either, but Erzua's band made me stronger and faster. I wouldn't be so easy to take down this time.

"And don't dive," Naomi went on. "That just gets you into trouble. Stay on your feet."

I waved a hand at her.

"Yeah, yeah," I said impatiently. "Don't worry. I've got Erzua's magic on my side."

My sister cocked her head at me. "What do you mean?" she asked.

"The band," I replied. "The one on my arm. You know, Erzua gave it to me."

Now it was Naomi's turn to wave a hand. She rolled her eyes, too.

"Oh, that?" she said, chuckling. "That melted days ago. The night we spent in North Village. Remember how warm it was in the barn? I thought you knew."

She scrunched up her nose. "You would have known if you took more baths."

Anything else she said was lost to me. I couldn't get past four small words.

That melted days ago.

That—the band—*melted days ago.*

I felt so dense! Erzua's band was gone. Lost! Most people would have noticed something like that.

"But … how?" I muttered.

How had I lifted Stormfall without the band? The hammer was too heavy, and I too weak. I was big, but not strong. How had I used it to battle the octoclops and

Ithasuma?

Naomi tapped her chest the way Ian had after our victory in the tower.

"You did it," she said, still tapping. "From in here. *Carpe draco,* Noah. I thought you knew that, too."

My mouth worked and my brain churned. She was telling me something important, but I couldn't quite get it.

"Game on!" the rule judge shouted. It was time to begin playing.

Still thinking, I jogged onto the field. Bart met me at the center line, all scowls and sneers.

"You're goin' down first, Naomi," he snarled at me. "No messin' around this time. Har, har!"

Same old Bart, I thought. He never changed, not unless getting hairier counted as change.

But I, on the other hand, had changed. Since our last meeting, I had lifted my father's hammer, defeated a mind-sucking monster, and become a hero.

Who would have thought a helpless big-boned nobody could do those things?

No one, of course, and that was what Naomi had been trying to tell me. The big-boned nobody didn't exist. He certainly wasn't me.

On our adventure, I had proven that I could be strong, courageous, and a good big brother. Not bad for a kid who had wrongly believed that he couldn't lift a hammer. I was better than I had ever imagined.

In honor of Ian, I called that becoming aware of the wolf. Ian had discovered that he really was a werewolf. He discovered it and accepted it. Being himself was better than being anyone else.

The same was true of me. I had become aware of the wolf—*my* wolf. We all had one inside. No, I wasn't going to howl at the moon or start chasing my tail. I just knew who I really was.

Everyone should be so lucky. When we quit worrying about who we weren't, the person inside us was all right.

So when Bart was given the Winter Orb to start the game, it ended differently than he'd hoped.

"Here it comes!" he roared, aiming straight for me.

Skree-ee-ee!

He threw and I dodged easily. The Orb whisked past my hip and struck a player behind me on the foot.

Poor Levi, I thought. He was always getting what Bart meant for me.

I scooped up the Orb before anyone else could reach it. This game was mine. Bart was mine.

"*Carpe draco,* Levi," I told my friend as he froze. Today is payback. Then I pivoted, drew back my arm, and threw.

Bart squealed but he couldn't avoid my perfect strike.

Skree-ee-ee!

The End

Knightscares Adventures

#1: Cauldron Cooker's Night
#2: Skull in the Birdcage
#3: Early Winter's Orb
#4: Voyage to Silvermight
#5: Trek Through Tangleroot
#6: Hunt for Hollowdeep
#7: The Ninespire Experiment
#8: Aware of the Wolf

More Adventures Coming Soon!

Want Free Knightscares ?

Join the Official Knightscares Fan Club Today!

Visit www.knightscares.com

*Read the latest news straight from the authors,
Charlie and David.*

*Join the Free Fan Club
Get Your Name on the Knightscares Website
Preview Upcoming Adventures
Invite the Authors to Your School
Lots More!*

Knightscares Artwork Winners

The artists will receive free autographed copies of Knightscares #8: Aware of the Wolf.

Alex (age 10) & Sean (age 9)
Maumee, OH

Kirston
Webberville, MI

The Trio From
Lake Leelanau, MI

Send Drawings To:
Knightscares Artwork
P.O. Box 654
Union Lake, MI   48387

Find out about the Knightscares Fan Art Contest at
www.knightscares.com

Great Work! Thank You!

Aware of the Wolf Artwork

The hand-painted cover art, official Knightscares logo, maps, and interior illustrations were all created by the talented artist Steven Spenser Ledford.

Steven is a free-lance fine and graphic artist from Charleston, SC with nearly 20 years experience. His work includes public and private wall murals, comic book pencil, ink and color, magazine illustrations and cover art, t-shirt designs, sculptures, portraits, painted furniture and more. Most of his work is produced from the tiny rooms of the house he shares with his very patient wife and their two children—Xena (a psychotic tortoise-shell cat) and Emma (a Jack Russell terrier). He welcomes inquiries at PtByNmbrs@aol.com.

Thank you, Steven!